MEMORY'S
SHADOW

We gratefully acknowledge the support of the Canada Council for the Arts and the Ontario Arts Council for our publishing program. We also acknowledge the financial support of the Government of Canada.

This is a work of fiction. Unless otherwise stated, all the names, characters, places, events and incidents in this book are either the product of the author's imagination or used in a fictitious manner. Any resemblance to actual persons, living or dead is purely coincidental.

Cover design: Val Fullard

Library and Archives Canada Cataloguing in Publication

Title: Memory's shadow : a novel / Gail Benick.
Names: Benick, Gail, 1945- author.
Series: Inanna poetry & fiction series.
Description: Series statement: Inanna poetry & fiction series
Identifiers: Canadiana (print) 20210162791 | Canadiana (ebook) 20210162813 | ISBN 9781771337816
   (softcover) | ISBN 9781771337823 (EPUB) | ISBN 9781771337830 (PDF)
Classification: LCC PS8603.E5567 M46 2021 | DDC C813/.6—dc23

Printed and Bound in Canada.

Published in Canada by
Inanna Publications and Education Inc.
210 Founders College, York University
4700 Keele Street, Toronto, Ontario M3J 1P3
Telephone: (416) 736-5356 Fax (416) 736-5765
Email: inanna.publications@inanna.ca Website: www.inanna.ca

MEMORY'S SHADOW

a novel

Gail Benick

inanna poetry & fiction series

INANNA PUBLICATIONS AND EDUCATION INC.
TORONTO, CANADA

For Luciana Ricciutelli-Costa (1958 – 2020)

Feminist visionary

Don't Iron While the Strike is Hot.

Women's Strike for Equality March on Fifth Avenue
New York City
August 26, 1970

The past is another country, but it has left its mark on those who once lived there.

Eric Hobsbawm, Interesting Times: A Twentieth-Century Life

Part I
Reunion

1972

Linda Sue

LATER, AFTER BLUEBERRY PANCAKES, they stood squeezed together, eyes fixed on her grave a couple of feet away. The wind brushed against their shivering bodies, lulling them into a reverie, brief and unsustainable.

"Remember how Mama always told us to keep our necks covered?" Hetty asked, pulling her paisley shawl tightly around her shoulders. In her hand, tucked out of sight, she squeezed a few pebbles to place on their sister's tombstone. *Terry Sue Berk, 1946 – 1963.*

"Mama and her crazy *shtetl* wisdom," said Tilya, who preferred to be called Toni when she wasn't with family. She detested how her mother had never left the house without something knotted at her throat—a silky square or a fringed oblong—plus two or three other scarves crammed into the unzipped section of her pocketbook. Just in case, she'd say. In case of what? Nobody knew.

Tilya wore nothing around her neck, never did, despite years of her mother's *kvetching*. The only scarves she would wear had to be handmade by a peasant women's collective in the Himalayan Mountains; it was important to her that her scarves simultaneously serve as a vehicle for strengthening gender identity and economic independence.

"Did Terry Sue like scarves?" Linda Sue asked. No one answered. "Well, she really didn't have much of a neck for scarves, did she?" Linda Sue pulled up the oversized collar of her navy pea coat and shoved her raw hands into the deep vertical side pockets designed, she wanted to believe, especially for her forlorn, chilled fingers. With Terry Sue gone, there was no buffer between her and her two older sisters. They had both been born in Poland, and their shared birthplace sometimes felt like a bond between them that excluded her. Still, it pained her now to admit that her beloved big sisters, her fashion consultants, had little in common except their place of birth.

"Right," Tilya said. She studied Hetty and Linda Sue for a moment, convinced that their graveside reunion was a mistake. A colossal miscalculation. "Terry Sue had no neck for scarves until a doctor surgically sculpted a slender, alabaster column for her by slicing off her extra fold of skin. That's the plain truth. Don't tell me you've forgotten."

"Of course I haven't forgotten," Hetty said, glaring at Tilya. "And don't you forget that she was only thirteen years old when she had that operation." Hetty stepped away from her sisters to place one of the pebbles on Terry Sue's headstone. She paused midway to look back at Tilya and Linda Sue standing there, sombre and trembling in winter's grip. Outside the cemetery, there were very few cars travelling east or west on Olive Boulevard; there wouldn't be much traffic on such a bleak Sunday afternoon in suburban St. Louis when most people were parked comfortably in front of their televisions.

"Enough already about Terry Sue's neck," Hetty said to Tilya. Her voice was sharp, but all three of them knew her anger wasn't about the shape of their deceased sibling's neck at all, but rather about the enduring pain from the loss of Terry Sue, their fragile sister, once the protected third child in a family of four daughters. Their grief continued to join them together, but also split them apart.

"Here we go again," Tilya said. "I knew coming here was going to be a disaster." She dropped her head forward, a little sullen, but also hurting. All she was able to bring back of Terry Sue was her strawberry-blonde hair and eager-to-please smile. Tilya unfurled Hetty's clenched fist and took a pebble to place on Terry Sue's headstone.

In place of a pebble, Linda Sue pulled an almond biscotti from her coat pocket. She had bought the biscotti at the bakery that morning because the dry, crunchy biscuit resembled Mama's *mandelbrot*. Terry Sue had loved the *mandelbrot*, before she stopped eating.

"Enjoy, my cutest sister," Linda Sue said in a whisper. "We'll always be joined by having the same middle name." She put the almond biscotti on the headstone. "And eat your *mandelbrot* quickly before the birds take it far, far away. Maybe somewhere warm, like Argentina."

"Where to?" Hetty asked as they walked in silence along the path leading to the cemetery gates. The chunky heels of Hetty's suede boots clicked against the slabs of pavement rife with weeds and stray blades of grass. The boots, skin tight and calf high, looked like they belonged on the feet of a European runway model.

Linda Sue touched Tilya's arm to slow her pace. "What's the big hurry?" she asked.

"Do you want the long answer or the short one?" Tilya responded.

Linda Sue had expected them to linger at their sister's grave; she had pictured them huddled together telling stories about Terry Sue—the time she cut off the horn of her stuffed unicorn, transforming it into a plush horse and the family car crash when Terry Sue's new ceramic mug bearing a puppy decal had been pulverized in the trunk.

"Well," said Hetty as they approached her car, "let's go somewhere Terry Sue would have liked." She unlocked and opened the car doors to allow fresh air to circulate inside. The car smelled of cigarettes from the client she had driven around that morning in search of the perfect, affordable house. Linda Sue climbed into the backseat, the sole of her shoe creasing the real estate listings that carpeted the floor. Ever since the family's head-on collision years ago, she couldn't ride in the front passenger seat, not even in her sister's luxury Oldsmobile—scrupulously serviced and maintained by her orthodontist husband Lenny—without yelping at the driver to stop or brake or slow down or something else irritating and inappropriate.

"Okay. Terry Sue really liked the zoo," Linda Sue said from her position in the back seat. She noticed that the dark roots of Hetty's auburn-tinted hair were beginning to show at the crown, and a few strands of grey wiggled out of Tilya's loose braid. "Or we could just drive around to show Tilya that U. City hasn't changed a bit since she left."

"Uh..." Tilya stalled. She dreaded what was coming next. They'd spend the afternoon cruising in and out of side streets, having conversations that would begin with, *"Remember that gorgeous guy who..."* and end with, *"You know, he became a bigtime lawyer in...."* If she was supposed to care, well, sorry. She didn't. "C'mon," she said. "No place is the same as it once was."

"Wrong, Tilya," Hetty shot back. "U. City is the same. I have clients who would give anything to live on Cornell Avenue or Princeton."

Tilya raised her eyebrows, always skeptical of any observation that came from the stodgy mind of her older sister.

"And if we're going to the zoo, I'd like to take Papa with us," Hetty said.

⁕

It took less than fifteen minutes to drive from the cemetery to Papa's house on Tulane Avenue where he had lived alone since Mama had died not long after Terry Sue's death. Hetty visited him daily; Linda stopped by weekly; and Tilya was such an infrequent visitor that her trips home were greeted with great jubilation, as if Catherine the Great had risen from her gold coffin in St. Petersburg and honoured her distant relatives with a brief stopover in St. Louis, MO. On each visit, Tilya saw new signs of deterioration. This time she noticed, as they approached the house, that the wooden front door looked warped. Several more shingles from the roof were missing. Nothing structural, Hetty would tell clients several years later when they asked about the interior cracks surrounding some of the windows. Nothing that a good coat of paint and some spackling couldn't fix, she'd assure them, though the sisters would ultimately come to an unspoken agreement: they would sell below market value instead of hiring workers to do the painting and spackling. Their father was too fragile to withstand the disruption.

Papa opened the door as soon as he heard their plotless chatter on the front porch. He'd been waiting, always waiting, to see his daughters, counting down days and then hours. What happened in between, he barely noticed. Papa stood at the door, wrapped in a crocheted blanket which he wore the way old men at shul wore prayer shawls—draped over their shoulders with the four corners hugging their hunched bodies.

"How are you, Papa?" Hetty leaned in to kiss him on the forehead and frowned when she heard wheezing coming from his chest. "Would you like a cup of tea with your three favourite girls?"

"A little tea, okay," he said, coughing. A shiny dot of pink phlegm landed in his handkerchief.

"We're going to the zoo, Papa. Want to come with us?" Linda Sue asked. He had often taken them to the zoo in Forest Park on Sundays to see the pandas and elephants. If an animal show happened to be scheduled for that afternoon (which happened often), they would stay to watch the lions or chimpanzees do their stunts. Tilya, when she joined them, never failed to rage against chimps dressed in frilly clothes, riding mini-bikes and walking on stilts. "Who," she would rant, "benefits from this idiocy?" And she didn't care that such visiting dignitaries as Red Skelton and Babe Ruth came to see the animal performers or that *Life* magazine labelled the St. Louis Zoo one of the most entertaining ever created in the USA.

Seeing her father's sunken face now, Tilya felt a twinge of guilt. She put her arms around her father's waist and lightly kissed his cheek. "Hello, Papa," she said. "Long time no see."

They sat at the dining room table drinking tea with lemon from glass mugs. Papa held a sugar cube under his tongue to sweeten the hot drink until he started coughing, this time more intensely. Hetty said, "You can go to the zoo with us next time, Papa. It's too cold for you today." Tilya looked away. For a millisecond, her father's persistent cough propelled her into a future she did not want to enter.

"Did my adorable son Josh come by to see you today?" Hetty asked, attempting to escape the subject of the zoo.

"Adorable? That kid is *meshuggah*," Papa said, setting off a round of laughter.

"All of a sudden he wants to go to Poland because he found some photos of the Lodz ghetto during World War II in a book."

"What's so crazy about that?" Linda Sue asked. "Maybe he wants to see where the Berkowitz family came from, you know, before they became the Berks. He's not a baby anymore."

Papa cupped his fingertips on his forehead and shook his head. "And what do you think Josh would find in Lodz?"

"I mean," said Linda Sue, "will someone in this family please decide if we are entitled to know how you and Mama managed to survive in the ghetto when Hetty and Tilya were little girls? It's like Lodz happened but didn't happen," she blurted. "Could you just make up your mind already and stop with all the secrets?"

Papa locked his shoulders in an uncertain shrug, his face contorted. He pushed himself away from the table, as if he hadn't heard Linda Sue's plea. "Papa," she said with more insistence. "Please tell me."

Hetty touched Papa's arm and offered to help him go upstairs for a nap. Linda Sue watched him hobble across the room. She listened to his breath become more laboured as his slippers shuffled along the matted rug. A surge of disappointment tightened in her chest. Her throat felt choked with sadness. She looked away, unable to beg him again. At the bottom of the stairs, Papa's hand, taut with bulging greyish veins, gripped the banister. Hetty cradled his emaciated torso in her arm and guided him up to his bedroom, removed the crocheted blanket from his shoulders, and tucked him into bed.

"*Nu*," he grumbled as he closed his eyes. "My only grandson needs his head examined."

◈

Tilya felt she had been home for days, but only forty-five minutes had passed since their arrival at her childhood home on Tulane Avenue. She had no desire to finish her tepid tea. The honey cake on the plate in front of her didn't tempt her in the least. Out of boredom, she circled her finger around the plate's rim, feeling a craggy chip that may have broken off years ago or yesterday. Whenever she stepped across the Berk threshold, she felt unsure whether she was moving backwards or standing still. Linda Sue was clearing the table and putting the unused lemon wedges into the fridge. The water from the kitchen tap sputtered as she rinsed the dishes. Tilya remained seated in the dining room, slumped in her chair, as if a vacuum cleaner had sucked the energy out of her. Dust covered the surface of Mama's sideboard, a thick layer that must have been collecting there for weeks.

As soon as Hetty returned from Papa's bedroom, Tilya proposed a new plan. "Forget the zoo," she said. "Let's drive downtown." For the first time that afternoon, her voice sounded buoyant, almost alive.

"No way," said Hetty. "Lenny would have a fit if he knew I drove downtown. In the Oldsmobile Starfire! Are you kidding?"

"Tilya," said Linda Sue, "It's too…"

"Dangerous? Is that what you were going to say?" Tilya rolled her eyes and pursed her lips in annoyance. She began to drum her fingers on the table, irked by her sisters' unbending, boring blandness.

"Look, Tilya," said Hetty, "you don't know everything. You think you're so smart, but actually, you're really, really not."

"I insist," Tilya said. "We're going."

"Yes, sir," said Linda Sue, saluting her sister. "At your command, boss. So, how do we get there?"

"You don't know, and you've lived here how long?" Tilya retorted. "Only your entire life."

"People get shot in broad daylight down there," Hetty said. "Honestly, Tilya, I'm scared to drive around in St. Louis."

"I've survived in New York for all these years. Come on!" She winked at Hetty. "We're survivors, after all. Besides, I promise I won't tell Lenny, okay? It'll be our secret.…"

"I'll drive," said Linda Sue.

"Not the Starfire, you won't," Hetty said. "Lenny would have a fit."

Tilya grabbed her coat. "Let's go," she said. "I need to be at Wash U. in a couple of hours." She strode out the door, not wanting to give Hetty time to change her mind.

As Hetty started to shut the door, she turned to Linda Sue. "Quick," she said. "Go check the stove. God forbid there should be a fire."

⁂

Hetty knew only one way to get downtown: Delmar Boulevard. Maybe there was a faster, shorter route, but she felt comfortable with what was familiar. It was entirely possible that she could drive through the U. City portion of Delmar, the prime stretch with its affluent homes and a secluded park, in her sleep. When they crossed into St. Louis proper around Skinker, she began to fidget with the heating in the car. Her hands felt sweaty on the steering wheel. Despite the upgraded leather interior, the seats felt stiff. "Are your doors locked?" she asked. Derelict buildings and vacant lots with patches of rubble appeared more frequently as they drove east. A few straggly dandelion seed heads dotted the empty spaces. "Roll up your windows," she commanded. "Do it right now or I'm turning back!"

"Not yet," Tilya said. "At least go as far as Jefferson Avenue." She was sitting in the front passenger seat, thinking about how to get to the neighbourhood north of Delmar in downtown St. Louis, the poor black area that had recently become famous—infamous, she silently corrected herself—because of a large housing project located there. "I want to see where Pruitt–Igoe is," she announced. "Then we can go have a chocolate malt at Crown Candy Kitchen. It's right around there."

"Tilya, you would want to see Pruitt–Igoe," said Hetty. "It's so unsafe around the housing project that no sane person wants to come downtown. But what do you care about our safety?" She glanced in her side mirror and made an illegal U-turn. The front tires of the Starfire hit the curb on the opposite side of the street.

Linda Sue felt her stomach lurch. "Let me out of here," she whimpered, but Hetty wasn't listening. Determined to return her family to the protective cocoon of U. City, she nervously flicked on her headlights.

"For god's sake, Hetty. Why on earth do you need your lights on at three-thirty in the afternoon?" Tilya demanded. "Forget the malts. Just drop me off at Wash U.. I'll find my own way home."

Hetty pulled the Starfire away from the curb with all the force she could summon. She stepped on the gas pedal, going recklessly fast, as if she were bolting out of the bowels of hell rather than leaving downtown St. Louis on an uneventful Sunday afternoon in February.

Tilya broke the silence in the car. After several minutes observing the desolate streets through her open window, she said cryptically, "Now I understand why planners call the city of St. Louis an island unto itself."

Hetty asked Tilya for the second time to roll up her window.

Linda Sue asked Hetty for the second time to slow down.

"You know, Papa once worked in a garment factory not far from here," Linda Sue reminded Tilya.

"So he did," she conceded. Before long they reached the city limit, the not-insignificant boundary dividing city and county. As they drove along the westerly edge of Forest Park, Tilya knitted her shapeless eyebrows together. "I've been thinking lately," she began. Warm air gushed from the car heater. The entrance to Washington University on Forsyth Boulevard was only minutes away. "I'm thirty-two," Tilya stated in a forthright tone, as if someone in the family was disputing her age. "And single."

"Well, you're hardly a spinster," Hetty said. Tilya wondered (to herself, for once) if her sister's knowledge of the housing market gave her some privileged insight into the marriage market, too.

"I wouldn't say you're a full-fledged cat lady just yet," Hetty added. She knew, of course, that Papa regarded his unmarried thirty-two-year-old daughter as a family embarrassment. A *shanda*, a shame, he would mutter whenever Tilya's name was mentioned.

"I'm obviously nearing the end of the peak years for marriage and child-bearing," Tilya said. Her bluntness left little room for argument. "Anyway, those factors notwithstanding, I've decided to have a child."

Hetty exchanged a stunned look with her youngest sister in the rearview mirror.

"So who's the lucky guy you're going to have this baby with?" Linda Sue asked.

"You'll be the first to know when the time comes," Tilya said as she lifted her briefcase onto her lap. "But I'll tell you right now. I'm not convinced that it's automatically wrong to raise a child without a man or a father in the house." Leaving her sisters dumbstruck, she opened the door of the Starfire. "But if you're so ridiculously concerned about my single mother proposition," she said to them, "just do what great women have always done. Write it down. Virginia Woolf was still writing in her diary until four days before she committed suicide."

"Good to know," said Linda Sue.

"Am I supposed to know who this Virginia Woolf lady is?" Hetty asked.

"Thanks for the ride," Tilya said without explaining who Virginia Woolf was. "By the way, I'm leaving a couple of notebooks on the front seat for you both to write down your thoughts, you know, like Virginia Woolf did. Trust me, keeping a diary is good for you." Hetty and Linda Sue watched their sister stride across campus toward the Olin Library, where she was meeting colleagues before her visiting lecture. As she walked, their sister made the transition from Tilya, daughter of Holocaust survivors, to Toni, professor of Women's Studies. (The nickname Toni, she'd lie to anyone who asked, was short for Antonia, pronounced in the English way with the accent on the second syllable.)

Before Hetty drove away, Linda Sue climbed into the front passenger seat, dutifully claiming the notebook with the blue cover as her diary. That left the green one for Hetty. Tilya had taken the red notebook with her.

◈

February 13, 1972

Dear me,

Tilya and her great ideas. Going downtown. Yikes! Did she want to get us murdered or something? And what about Crown Candy? That chocolate malt she promised? Nope. Didn't happen. Not even a single piece of bubble gum. The whole thing was crazy. Just like Tilya's decision to have a baby. Is she out of her mind? Where does she get these insane ideas from? Of course, after such a weird day, I had the weirdest dream. It was about a phone call from Terry Sue. You know, I hardly ever dream about her. Nine years is a long time to be gone. She didn't say where she was calling from, but she told me that Mama was making a fresh batch of *mandelbrot* just for her. It figures.

Now here's the part of the dream that doesn't make sense to me. Instead of asking about Papa or Mama or her stuffed animals or something she would have known about when she was alive, she said, "Is Tilya really going to have a baby?" Isn't that a weird question? How would Terry Sue have known that Tilya wanted to have a kid? Before I could answer, Terry Sue went on: "Tilya never even liked children or me all that much." Then I woke up. Just like that.

Toodle-oo for now,
LS.

Toni

TONI ENTERED OLIN LIBRARY, a modern, window-dominated structure, too airy and new to have that musty library smell of decaying paper, ink, and glue. Even on Sunday, late in the afternoon, Olin teemed with students clambering up and down the wide staircase, like kinetic sculptures making soft, chirpy sounds. Olin opened in 1962, Toni's last year as an undergrad at Wash U., and it had never become a sanctuary for her in the way that Ridgley Hall was. There, in the serenity of the gothic main reading room, she had allowed herself to cry when Terry Sue was hospitalized for anorexia. She had imagined stashing an archive of Terry Sue's letters somewhere in Ridgley Hall. They had been written as her sister wasted away in the Missouri State Mental Hospital. It was just a fantasy she had once entertained, a way to give Terry Sue's life a lasting meaning.

Now, stepping inside Olin, Toni unfastened the top two buttons of her coat and pulled off her gloves. She exaggerated the gestures in order to separate herself from the strained car ride with Hetty and Linda Sue, revisiting briefly that odd feeling of being connected and not connected to them. Maybe the library was still a refuge from family turbulence, Toni thought. She didn't believe in God, not in the least. But she did believe in books and libraries.

About half a dozen women greeted Toni in the atrium, all

sheathed in black, managing somehow to look modest and bold at the same time. (They would continue to wear black for the next forty years, but exude less modesty and more *chutzpah* as the decades rolled on.) Her friends Lucinda and Noreen had flown in from San Diego, and her upstate friends Marilyn, Jo, and Samantha had come from Ithaca to share their research findings. Education consultant, Olivia, was there from Philly. Pioneers of Women's Studies, they would all surely support her plan to head up a single-parent family. Better still, they would applaud her for it. These sisters, her colleagues and comrades, would not respond with shocked faces the way Hetty and Linda Sue had. Toni knew exactly what they had been thinking. She could read the look that passed between her siblings in the rearview mirror; she could hear their judgment, without a word spoken. The message was clear and direct: Mama would turn over in her grave if she knew.

Outside the circle of friends stood someone who was watching and listening to the animated greetings of these seven women. The outsider had a tall, large frame, tightly coiled hair, and a pensive look on her face—and she was the only Black person in the atrium. Later, she joined Toni's seminar on gender role stereotyping and androgyny, a concept, they unanimously agreed, that reflected the perfect blending of masculine and feminine traits into a new human type. Alice, a psychologist and rising academic star, tossed her long unkempt pigtails over her shoulders. "There are not two sexes," she declared, "but rather a spectrum of individual proclivities more or less male and more or less female." Nodding in agreement, Lucinda stated that the shift to a service-oriented economy required more androgyny. She passed around copies of an article she had recently written on the overrepresentation of women in the retail sector, apologizing for the staples that pierced the text on the front pages of some photocopies.

Marilyn, the lone historian in the group, added, "We're going to need more deviation from the two-sex framework if our culture is to survive." Off and on, Toni coughed.

Sipping orange juice from an aluminum can, she quipped hoarsely, "Androgyny is becoming almost as American as, well..." She paused, then flashed back to Terry Sue's pancake-flat chest and the menstrual blood that never flowed. "It's true. Androgyny is becoming as American as protests, the silent majority, and mom's apple pie," Toni said. "But, trust me. That's not the way it was in the fifties when I was growing up here."

When the evening was over, Toni leaned over to Lucinda, who was sitting on her right, yawning. "Who was the Black woman with us tonight?" Toni asked her. She had been aware of the woman's silence through most of the seminar.

"I'm not sure," Lucinda said. "I think she's in anthropology. She told me she was conducting interviews with people living at Pruitt–Igoe." Toni nodded but said nothing. "By the way, thank you for letting me stay at your father's place."

"My pleasure," Toni said. "But I've got to be honest: it's not The Ritz."

"Sounds fine, thanks," said Lucinda. "I'm not fussy."

Once they arrived home, Toni fumbled in her purse for her old house key to avoid ringing the doorbell and waking Papa. The house was so quiet when they entered that they could hear mice scampering in the attic. The pungent smell of chicken noodle soup from dinner hung heavily in the air. As they tiptoed up the stairs, they heard Papa's strained and coarse snoring, the sound of a life secured against the odds. Toni gave Lucinda her room, and she took Terry Sue's.

✦

February 14, 1972

Can't sleep. 2:08 a.m. Pink bedspread, dust ruffle still wrapped around the bedframe. Have the sheets ever been changed? At least they don't stink. But they're cold as the grave. Shit... I can't get back to sleep after that nightmare. I was bent over the bathtub of our house on Tulane bathing both of my younger sisters. Terry Sue was sitting closest to the spigot. Her hair was short, and I was trying to decide if she was a little boy or girl. Then Terry Sue tossed some bubbles from the bathwater at me and said, "Someday, Tilya, you are going to have a baby just like me." She stuck her tongue out as far as she could, shook her head, and squinted her eyes shut all at once.

So, okay. Maybe it was just a bad dream, but really, the longer I'm here in St. Louis, the more I realize that you can't go home again. Or at least I can't. It's no fun going back to a place that once smelled of Mama's fresh *mandelbrot*, but feels stale and stagnant whenever I return. And my sisters. Were they always so cautious and conservative? It's not that I don't care about Hetty and Linda Sue—of course I do. How could I not? They are my blood relatives. How many times did Mama tell me that blood is thicker than water? At least a million times. But I have a hell of a lot more in common with the sisters that I march with. They are my home now. Women of the world unite!

Yours in sisterhood,
Toni

Hetty

"**P**APA!" HETTY BEGGED. "Turn down the television." No matter what time of day or night she visited him, no matter the season, Hetty found her father reclining on the sofa, swaddled in his crocheted shawl with the television so loud it could be heard in Kansas. "You'll go deaf," she said, suppressing the fact that he already was hard of hearing. Yet, his hearing aids sat unused in the corner of his top dresser drawer. On the few days he remembered to insert the small bud-like contraptions into his ears, the batteries were usually dead. Hetty bent over to pick up the Saturday edition of the *Post Dispatch* that had slipped from Papa's lap. It was the third week in April and there was still no word from Tilya. She had returned to New York City to finish the winter teaching semester, leaving Hetty to fret over the embarrassing possibility of a Berk baby-naming ceremony before Tilya was married. Or maybe there would be no wedding at all. Perhaps her willful sister, the genius, would change her mind for the sake of the family's reputation. Sure she would, Hetty thought, and pigs can fly. The image of a bloated pink animal with a round snout floating in the sky seemed particularly alien and unattractive to her. She shook her head and tapped her father's shoulder. Startled by his daughter's presence, he sat upright on the sofa, his bald scalp dotted with brown spots resembling a speckled egg. She planted a kiss on the smooth surface.

Thumbing through the real estate section of the newspaper, Hetty noticed several well-priced listings in U. City. A two-storey brick house on Shaftesbury was featured as the Home of the Week, proof that U. City was still a desirable location for home buyers. So what if the Jewish population was beginning to move farther west? Let the Bernsteins move to Ladue and the Shmanskies relocate in Creve Coeur. The Berks were staying put even if the skin colour of their neighbours was beginning to change. We are not racists, she assured herself.

Hetty crossed the living room and cranked the rotary knob to the left on Papa's old Zenith television. Before the sound dissipated completely, she heard Walter Cronkite interrupt normal programming for a specially televised event. "We take you now to the north side of St. Louis where building C-15 of the Pruitt–Igoe housing project is about to be demolished less than twenty years after it was built."

Next to Cronkite, reporters and a *Life* magazine photographer were poised to document the imminent implosion. Hetty raced to the kitchen to phone Tilya in New York, to say, in so many words, I told you so. Pruitt–Igoe was obviously too crowded, too dirty, too crime-ridden for anyone to have a decent life there. Just ask a real estate agent. The only solution was to blast all thirty-three towers in the housing project out of existence and build something new. Something much more marketable, Hetty thought. She let the phone ring in New York four times—one ring to signify each Berk sister, dead or alive. Then she hung up and quickly called back. That way Tilya would know it was a long-distance call from the family. There was no answer at Tilya's and, most likely, no television at her place either.

Papa asked Hetty to turn up the sound on the Zenith. The CBS cameraman slowly panned the site of building C-15: broken windows, a thin layer of grass, the metal frame of a swing set with missing seats, and the parking lot sprinkled with shards of glass.

"Look familiar?" Hetty asked him.

"*Nu,*" he said. "I used to go downtown every day for work. I shouldn't know downtown St. Louis when I see it?"

"True," she said to her father, trying to halt the conversation as soon as she noticed Josh walking through the door. Linda Sue followed right behind him.

Papa continued. "Do you think ghettos were invented yesterday, Hetty?"

"Shush," Hetty said.

"You don't remember living in the Lodz ghetto?" Papa shook his head.

Josh and Linda Sue joined them as a reporter was interviewing one of the wreckers from the Loizeaux family, who had been contracted to demolish the building.

"Good Shabbos, Zaidie," Josh said, plunking his gangly body on the sofa next to his grandfather. "Got anything good to eat?"

"Go look in the icebox, Joshie," he said. "You don't need to see this."

"Zaidie," Josh said, "I've told you a hundred times. I'm not a baby anymore." He refused to budge while the demolition engineer described how they had drilled sixteen-inch-deep holes into the concrete pillars on the ground, on the first floor, and in two small basement areas in order to fit the dynamite in place. "Awesome," Josh said. "Why didn't we ever go downtown to see Pruitt–Igoe?"

"You sound just like your Aunt Tilya," Hetty chided him. "It's filled with gangs, drug dealers, murderers, broken toilets, garbage piled up, floods of raw sewage in the hallways. It's a ghetto, Josh."

"You should only know from ghettos," Zaidie muttered under his breath. He rose to his feet and planted himself directly in front of the television with his fingers entwined behind his back. "If only Lodz never had a Jewish ghetto. We should be so lucky."

"I'm going to Lodz," said Josh. "Aunt Linda is taking me for a bar mitzvah present. Right, Aunt Linda? You promised." Josh got up to stand next to Zaidie. One hundred and fifty-two dynamite charges had been put in place and were sequentially fired from within the building. Suddenly, the base supports of the building imploded, the floor plates shattered, and the brick façade cascaded down as a giant cloud of dust and debris puffed up from the ground. The force of the implosion knocked over walls. Steel doors looked like paper.

"Jesus H. Christ!" an onlooker cried out. "What the holy fuck just happened?"

"Man, that's sick," said another. "Never seen anything like it. Not around here."

The demolition sent shock waves through the crowd that had gathered to witness the cataclysm. Some were residents still living in the other Pruitt–Igoe towers surrounding building C-15. Other residents watched from their windows. The butcher from Irv's IGA around the corner was there in his blood-streaked apron, and so were representatives from the St. Louis Housing Authority. They were confident that this destructive act would somehow save the housing development and lead to its radical rehabilitation.

A tall Black woman with a briefcase slung across her shoulder walked into the motley gathering of witnesses and put her arm around one of the spectators. She wore a tailored blazer and soft leather pumps. The lens of the camera quickly followed the two of them.

"You were a resident of building C-15, were you not?" the woman with the briefcase asked a spectator. A CBS reporter sidled up to them and held his microphone in front of the two women, who were joined in a semi-embrace.

"Yes, ma'am, I was." She glanced at the pile of rubble that had been her home. The other spectators were beginning to disperse, some brushing off the residue of dust that had settled on their light spring clothes.

"How long did you live in Pruitt–Igoe?"

"I've lived here for about eleven years. A good long time." She shook her head in disbelief as she spoke.

"It's a real tragedy," the woman with the briefcase said, pulling the resident toward her so that she could speak directly into the CBS microphone.

"I'll tell you the truth, ma'am. I feel real sad. Pruitt–Igoe is our home. I can remember Christmas here with all the windows lit up with blue and yellow and red lights. I can remember children playing on the swings. I can remember the smell of cookies baking when I walked down the hallway to my apartment. My kids grew up here. They had friends here. They went to school near here. This was our home." Her shoulders slumped and her eyes glazed over with tears.

"How many children do you have?" the CBS reporter queried.

"I have five kids living with me in Pruitt–Igoe," the woman answered. She shook her head again.

"Where will you go now?" the woman with the briefcase asked.

"You know, we have to move for the time being to another building in this housing project until we can find somewhere else to live. I'll tell you the truth. They pulled our homes right out from under us."

"What will you miss about living here?" The CBS reporter stepped closer to the two women, positioning the microphone inches from their faces. Their robust bodies seemed attached at the hips.

"Oh, you know, I'll miss the good times we had. In the beginning, this place was so nice. Just like a palace in the sky. You know, people on the outside don't really see the true picture."

Hetty squeezed between her father and son to turn off the television. The rotary knob came off in her hand. "Josh," she said, "Go get pliers if you can find a pair around here so we can shut this damn thing off."

"Wait a minute," Linda Sue said. "Call Tilya. She has to see this."

The CBS reporter tilted the microphone in the direction of the woman with the briefcase, who appeared self-possessed despite the brick façade of building C-15 in ruins behind her.

"I already called Tilya. She's not home." Hetty said, leaving the living room. "And what's Pruit–Igoe got to do with her or the price of eggs anyway?"

On television, the CBS reporter asked the woman with the briefcase for a closing comment. "What America needs to understand," she said, "is that Pruitt–Igoe was a community. It was a neighbourhood for these people, and now they're nowhere." She bent over and slipped one of the rocks from the debris into her pocket.

Walter Cronkite moved quickly to wrap up the CBS coverage. "And that's the way it is," he said, "on Saturday, April 22, 1972."

Hetty yelled from the kitchen to turn off the damn television already. "The whole thing is giving me a migraine," she mumbled, swallowing a couple of Aspirin tablets with a glass of tap water.

⬧

April 25, 1972, 11:15 a.m.

Dear Diary,

I'm waiting in the car for my next client to arrive, a Mrs. Hersh who is looking for a three-bedroom with two baths and a finished basement. (She's already fifteen minutes late, which really pisses me off.) So I thought that I might as well give this diary thing a try. In a million years, it would never occur to me to keep a diary. Like I have nothing better to do. Tilya doesn't get it. She doesn't know how much time it takes to raise kids. No freaking idea. She'd rather be marching in some women's lib demonstration than packing lunches for school. Not to mention that I hate the avocado green cover of this stupid diary. Reminds me of a kitchen appliance. Yuk!

Well, when I left Papa's house the other day, I had one of my little panic attacks. The blow-up of that slum housing project downtown really scared me. At least Cronkite could have told the television viewers who Igoe and Pruitt were. He could have made the story more human, that's all.

As soon as Lenny and I finished dinner that night, I asked him about moving out of U. City. "The handwriting is on the wall," I said to him, but I didn't get the feeling he was paying much attention. So I said, "Well, where do you think all those homeless people from Pruitt–Igoe are going to live? Ferguson or right here in U. City." We went to bed early. Lenny started to kiss me. He slipped his hand under my nightgown and walked his fingers up to my breasts because that's what we usually do on Saturday night, but I let out a tiny *kvetch*. "You should have seen that housing project in the ghetto crumple, Lenny," I said. "Like a scar on the earth." After a few seconds he said, "Hmm," and then rolled over to his side of the bed. For at least twenty minutes, maybe more, I stared at the ceiling until my eyes drooped shut. And then I was back in the Lodz ghetto, standing in the courtyard of that wretched apartment where we were forced to live. Or die. I could still smell the shit from overflowing pails and sewage. A stray dog with every rib protruding pulled a dead baby out of the garbage. The dog gripped the baby's foot with its teeth and dragged the corpse away, like it was a Raggedy Ann doll. How in the hell did Tilya and I ever survive that nightmare?

So here's my client finally.

Wish me luck.

Always,
Hetty

Part II

Search

1976

Linda Sue

LINDA SUE SMOOTHED THE WRINKLES from the white tablecloth in Papa's dining room. She was helping to prepare for Shabbat dinner, a winter Shabbat on one of the darkest and coldest evenings of the season, when threats of global cooling and a new ice age seemed eminently possible. In such a climate, with weather experts predicting polar bears in Manhattan and penguins in Florida, a meal of heavy food, most of it salty and overcooked, felt particularly welcoming as they braced for another storm. Linda Sue walked into the kitchen where Josh and his younger sister, Stacey, were removing dishes and glassware from the cupboard to set the dining room table. As soon as Josh saw his aunt, he began needling her about the promised trip to Poland.

"I'll be ancient by the time you get around to organizing this thing, Aunt Linda," Josh taunted her.

"Okay, this summer for your high school graduation present," she said.

Hetty, bending over the oven to rustle the roasting potatoes in hot oil, listened to their banter. Each hour delaying their trip, every millisecond of postponement, felt triumphant to her. She dreaded the moment that Josh would leave for a country she wanted only to forget. Furthermore, none of her synagogue friends had teenage sons or daughters who were travelling behind the Iron Curtain. Maybe Linda Sue could chaperone Josh on a Grand Tour of Europe, like upper-crust Englishmen used to take when they finished their education at Oxford or Cambridge. Hetty was prepared to pay great sums of money for Josh to trek through France and Italy in search of art, culture, and the origins of Western civilization. She imagined his postcards from Paris, Venice, Rome, and Pompeii. He might even perfect his French and learn a bit of Italian. It never hurt to have more than one language, Mama had often advised her, because a girl never knew where she might end up.

For Linda Sue, the endless dithering—her own fault, she would be the first to admit—felt like madness. There was nothing more quirky, she was convinced, than the Berks' inability to make firm decisions and get on with it. Tilya couldn't figure out how to bring a baby into her life. Hetty couldn't decide whether to sell her house and move farther west. And she couldn't even plan a simple two-week holiday with her nephew. Reaching over Stacey's head for a wine goblet stored on the cupboard's top shelf, Linda Sue could barely grasp the fragile stem. The goblet slipped through her fingers and shattered. Josh began to pick up the pieces, but Hetty wouldn't let him or Stacey go anywhere near the slivers of glass. She feared—although she didn't dare to say it aloud—a bloodbath.

When Hetty rose to bless the Sabbath candles a bit later, her voice sounded weary. She kissed Josh and Stacey on the tops of their heads, lingering for a moment with her hands on their shoulders, hesitant to let go. Papa said the blessing over the *challah*, and then he pulled a small piece from the end of the twisted bread and salted it before he took a bite.

"*Gut Shabbos*, my *kinder*," he said.

"A-a-men," said Josh, holding a hunk of the yellow bread in his hand, the sesame seeds on the crust falling onto his plate. "This summer," he announced, "Aunt Linda is finally going to take me to Lodz. And no arguing. It's my grad present."

"I want to go, too," Stacey said. Her thick auburn curls were held back with a narrow headband, which made her look much younger than fifteen and drew attention to the dramatic V-shape in her hairline near the centre of her forehead.

"That's enough," Hetty said. She glanced several times at Lenny across the table, registering his increasing discomfort with the direction of the conversation. She knew that her husband would never allow both of their children to leave St. Louis with Linda Sue in search of the Berk family's elusive past. Absolutely not. Over the years, he had expressed a touch of skepticism regarding the family's survival in the Lodz ghetto during the war. He was frankly detached from all things European because his family came to the States in the previous century and regarded themselves as one-hundred percent American. Without being disrespectful, he wished the whole business of the Berks' past would go away. Papa frowned at Josh and shook his head in mild distress while Hetty set the charity box on the table. She gave Josh and Stacey a few coins to push through the opening at the top of the tin container. "You don't need to go to Poland to dredge up injustices from the past," she told Josh and Stacey. "Charity and good deeds start at home."

"That's like comparing chalk and cheese," Linda Sue said to Hetty.

"I don't get it," Stacey said. "What do chalk and cheese have to do with Poland?"

"Maybe the Berks were dairy farmers in Lodz," Josh said.

"Don't be ridiculous," Hetty corrected him. "Who was milking cows in the ghetto?"

Papa winced at his grandchildren's ignorance, the gaps in their understanding of his identity and his geography. They knew next to nothing of Warsaw or Lodz and even less about the *shtetls* in Poland, where Jews had lived long before the Holocaust—where, in fact, his own ancestors had roots. Yet, he listened and said nothing.

"Okay, Josh," Linda Sue said. "I'm going to start looking for cheap flights tomorrow. And a little information about Jews in Poland wouldn't hurt either." She rattled the charity box that had once held her own sweaty nickels and dimes.

✦

Three Shabbat dinners later, between the *gefilte* fish and *matzah* ball soup, Linda Sue announced the August dates for their Poland trip. It would be the first time any of their family members had stepped foot in the old country since the end of World War II. The response around the dinner table on Friday night was less than joyous. Linda Sue was not surprised. She herself felt overwhelmed. Every inquiry about trains in Poland forced her to picture what could have happened to Mama, Papa, Hetty, and Tilya. Each time she studied the map of Poland, she imagined the four of them hiding somewhere in a forest or a barn or cellar. As she searched for a tour guide, she wondered what a complete stranger would be able to tell her and Josh about the Berks' survival. This guide would have to be some sort of diviner. A magician pulling ghostly relatives out of a hat.

As their departure loomed closer and closer, Linda Sue resented the veil of secrecy cloaking the Berks' past more and more. She wished her family understood that their secrets caused her considerable pain. How could they not see that? Just before she finalized the purchase of the airplane tickets, she gave Tilya one last chance to divulge what she knew. Big mistake, Linda Sue thought, as soon as Tilya answered the phone in New York. Her flat, disinterested tone seemed to be reserved especially for her sisters.

"So, what's doing?" Tilya barely managed to ask after an awkward pause. The emotion in her voice was so tempered that Tilya could have been speaking to a brick wall.

"Not much," Linda Sue said. "Are you in the middle of something?" No matter how callous Tilya appeared, Linda Sue never stopped thinking of her as the family's brightest star, maybe even the Jonas Salk of women's studies. Who was she, Linda Sue, to interrupt her sister on the cusp of a big breakthrough in the study of androgyny? But she couldn't wait any longer for Tilya to become a national heroine. "You're sure you don't want to go to Poland with Josh and me this summer?" Linda Sue spoke as if this were a straightforward question rather than an indirect appeal for some sort of communion with her sister.

"Yep. Absolutely sure," Tilya said. "Is that why you called?"

"Sort of." Linda Sue sighed. "I just don't want any surprises when we get there, Tilya. Josh is still a pretty impressionable kid, you know."

"I'm well aware of my nephew's age and the way he's been shielded from the big bad world we live in." The phone line began to crackle. "And your point is?"

"It must be snowing or raining where you are, Tilya. There's so much static, I can hardly hear you. Anyway, if you could stop being such a cold cucumber for one second…" Her voice trailed off.

"I am not a cold cucumber," she pushed back. "It's just that I'm looking forward, not backward, like some people I know."

Linda Sue twirled her hair around her fingers, nervously, then licked her upper lip, which felt dry and in need of her misplaced ChapStick. The static on the phone line was becoming intolerable. "Well," she said to Tilya, "maybe, just maybe, a memory, even a tiny fragment from those times, still rattles in that head of yours. Would it be so terrible?"

"Actually, it would," Tilya replied. "I've got to go."

"But… how is your search for a baby going?"

"So so," Tilya said. "Listen, Linda Sue, I need to—"

"Wait. Don't hang up yet. I want to tell you one more thing."

"Make it fast."

"Well, all thirty-three buildings of Pruitt–Igoe are now gone," Linda Sue said. "Finito. Can you believe it?"

"I know," Tilya said. "It's terrible. My friend Marion from Wash U. told me about it. And lots of the people in those buildings were women. Single parents." With a flick of her wrist, she put down the receiver of the phone, leaving Linda Sue to wonder what just happened.

⁂

June 25, 1976

Dear me,

I'm so sick and tired of Tilya's smug attitude. Does she really believe that she is so superior just because she wants to liberate women? Like she's the only one who's ever tried to make the world a better place. Oh, sure. She should only know what my fifth graders are doing with their history projects on heroes. I'm clipping my lesson plan to this page in case my holier-than-thou sister ever gets her hands on my diary. She promised she wouldn't read it, but you never know what will happen. I've marked up my copy of the lesson plan with a few notes in parentheses just to show that I'm a very conscientious teacher, the best I can be. I, too, am saving the world in my own way, one student at a time.

Toodle-oo for now,
LS.

Lesson Plan

Brief Description

Students create an ABC book about heroes in history.

Objectives

Students research information about people in history that we recognize as heroes. Students write short biographies about their assigned heroes.

Keywords

Heroes, history, ABC book

Materials Needed

- library sources
- writing paper
- different coloured construction paper
- drawing paper
- glue
- scissors
- markers or crayons

- chalkboard and chalk or chart paper
- hole punch
- brass fasteners or loose-leaf rings (didn't have)

Lesson 1: 45 minutes

- Ask students to name famous people in history we recognize as heroes. (I told the kids a hero had to be someone with great strength and courage, someone who had done something brave or dangerous to help somebody else, someone who was so interesting and special that they would feel inspired by this person's actions even on the most boring, hottest, longest day of the summer.)
- Write students' responses on the board or on a chart. Ask students which names on the list they would include if they were going to write a book about different heroes. (Note to self. My fifth graders came up with George Washington, Abraham Lincoln, Martin Luther King, and Moses. But something incredible happened when I was teaching the lesson. One of the students asked me who my hero was. I didn't want to be too personal or too frivolous or too religious or too highbrow or lowbrow, so I said that my hero was a man that I had been reading about to prepare for my upcoming trip to Poland. I wrote his name on the board: Jan Korczak. "Who's he?" they all shouted. So I gave a brief description of Korczak because it was coming up to lunchtime. I told them that he was a pediatrician who was the director of an orphanage in Warsaw during a scary time. When he was ordered to send all of the orphans in his care to the train station where they would be taken to a camp, he told the children to dress in their

best clothes. Each child was given a blue knapsack and a book or a favourite toy to carry. Korczak marched with the children to the train station. "He got on the train," I told them, "and stayed with the children until the end when they all died because, well, because it was an unusual camp, a death camp." When the bell rang for lunch, nobody moved. "What do you mean 'death camp'?" Rosalind asked. She's such a quiet student usually. "I mean a camp where they put Jews to death," I said. I was trying to be gentle. "Not the children, though!" Rosalind said. "Even the children..." Rosalind put her head in her hands, sobbing. Barry, the class barracuda, said he would kill those bad guys at that terrible death camp. What have I done? What if these impressionable kids go home and tell their mothers I told them about camps where children were put to death? I could lose my job. Worse still. I could frighten these kids. (I'd rather be dead than hurt them.)

- Write the letters of the alphabet on the board. Check off the letters associated with names suggested by students. (I included my suggestion.)
- Tell students that they are going to create their own ABC book of heroes. The book will include some names on their suggested list plus others that are added to complete the alphabet. (Korczak didn't make the final cut.)
- Assign each student a letter. Students will research a hero in history whose last name begins with that letter.
- Have students write a short biography about the person and draw a picture of the person.
- Give students a few days to complete their research, write their biographies, and draw the illustrations.

Lesson 2: 45 minutes

- Let students paste their biographies and pictures onto different coloured construction paper. Let one or two students arrange the pages in alphabetical order. Ask students to create a title for the book. (My kids chose "You Are My Hero." Pretty good for fifth graders.)
- Punch two or three holes on one side of each page. Assemble the pages using brass fasteners or loose-leaf rings.

Suggestion: To extend the life of the book, laminate or put clear contact paper on the cover. Put the book in the school learning centre. (I plan to use this lesson plan next year and for many years in the future.)

Hetty

ETTY SAT AT HER KITCHEN TABLE with *Tidy Tips from Trish* open in front of her. Between preparing for the move and getting Josh ready for the trip to Poland, Hetty was beside herself. She squabbled with Lenny over the most minor transgressions, like burying his head in the newspaper at breakfast. She promised herself to leave their house in U. City spotless. That was the advice she always gave her clients. Do unto others, she'd remind them at the close of a sale. Now Hetty felt obliged to throw away the broken Sunbeam Mixmaster that had cluttered her kitchen counter for nearly three years, along with junk mail, articles cut from various newspapers, and various promotional flyers. Westward ho! "Frontenac, here we come," she said aloud with a shudder of excitement, though the truth was she felt anxious about being twenty-eight minutes away from Papa. Actually it was less than that in off-peak hours. She pictured the new house. It represented her dream of "making it in America," which she had aspired to for her whole life. Something about a colonial style house in Frontenac gave her the feeling that she had finally arrived. She loved the kitchen peninsula and ceramic tile floors, the formal dining room, the panelled den and, the crowning glory, the built-in microwave.

Flipping through the pages of *Tidy Tips* while sipping her late afternoon cup of tea, Hetty paused on the topic of pillows.

Trish advised smart women to replace tattered, worn-out pillows when moving up in the world. "Good advice, Trish," Hetty murmured into her teacup. She wondered whether Trish, a name she adored, was the author's real name. It sounded to her like the name of a character in one of her *True Romance* magazines, which she vowed to dump before the move. The whole lot of them. Or maybe it was short for Patricia, a name she adored much less. But any given name was better than Hetty, which her clients often confused with Betty. Hetty sounded all wrong for someone who was going to live in an elegant home in Frontenac. It was a name for a servant in that kind of a house, she thought, tapping her toe nervously on the linoleum in her kitchen.

The *Tidy Tips* section on crayons caught Hetty's attention. *If you have a young Picasso who has scribbled on the walls, here's the quick fix: dry-cleaning solvent. Pour a bit on a terry-cloth towel to safely remove crayon marks from almost any surface except antique wallpaper.* There were no crayon marks on any of her walls, and Hetty had never papered her home with antique wallpaper. In fact, Stacey was so disinclined to draw that Hetty believed her daughter would not know what to do with a crayon if one were placed between her thumb and her forefinger. However, Stacey had inherited her mother's love of fashionable clothes and her inability to get rid of a single item. Skirts, dresses, sweaters and blouses invariably carpeted every inch of Stacey's floor.

Josh's room was another matter. His walls were also free of crayon marks. But, her son, the budding photographer, used Scotch Tape to affix all of his photos to the walls. She wished Trish had a quick and cheap solution for that. Well, here's to new beginnings, she said to herself, emptying her tasteless tea down the sink.

A foul smell from the dishwasher hit her. Hetty instinctively reached for her *Tidy Tips*. She was searching the index when Linda Sue appeared at the back door.

"Glad you're here," Hetty said. "Something stinks in the dishwasher."

Linda Sue walked over to the old appliance and took a sniff. "Yep. It smells. Got any vinegar? That'll work."

"Good advice." She went to the cabinet to find a bottle of pure distilled white vinegar. "Now you can tell me what to do with Stacey. She's sulking in her bedroom because she can't go to Poland with you and Josh. Can you talk to her?"

"Okay. I'll give it a try." Linda Sue left the kitchen and started up the stairs for her niece's room. "Hey, Hetty," she yelled. "Check the bottom of the dishwasher for bits of food and gunk before you douse it with vinegar."

Stacey was reclining on a heap of throw pillows propped against her headboard as Linda Sue entered her bedroom. She barely lifted her eyes and offered no greeting.

"Tough times, sweetheart?" Linda Sue asked. She glanced at the poster-size photo of Stacey hanging over the bed. The picture, taken on Stacey's first birthday, had captured her as a bouncy, curly-haired child. She was wearing a white cotton dress with box pleats, a piped Peter Pan collar, and four paired cherries yo-yo-stitched down the front. Hetty was so taken with the cherry dress—its timeless simplicity and touch of class, she'd always comment—that she preserved it forever in a gilded wood frame that hung on the opposite wall.

"Only my crazy sister Hetty would frame a baby dress," Linda Sue said to Stacey. "Is it going to Frontenac with you?"

"Definitely not in my room," she said.

"Well, you know that John F. Kennedy Jr. wore the short pants version when he was a little boy, and that cherry dress is still the Easter holiday uniform for families who belonged to exclusive places like the St. Louis Country Club."

Stacey didn't respond.

"You know, the history of the cherry dress is quite interesting."

"Not interested," Stacey said. She was sitting upright in a nest of blankets, unwilling to meet her Aunt Linda's eyes. A song from Grease ripped through her stereo speakers. "My mom bought it somewhere, but I really don't care."

"Well, darling, there's only one shop in the whole world that sells the cherry dress. It's the Woman's Exchange of St. Louis on Clayton Road, not far from your new house." Linda Sue paused to see if Stacey was listening. She wasn't.

"So?"

"So you might find the Woman's Exchange interesting. It's been in business since 1883."

"Thanks for that great information, but like I'm really not interested." Stacey flopped backwards.

"Okay, I get the message," Linda Sue said, "but you should ask Aunt Tilya about how the Woman's Exchange helped destitute women earn a living."

"Sorry. Not interested," Stacey said. "I don't even know what destitute means."

"It means poor. They were penniless single women, often divorced. Working from home."

"Enough already," Stacey retorted. She picked up a crushed Kleenex lying on her bed and blew her nose.

"They worked at home so the neighbors didn't see them going out to work. So nobody would know they needed to work. Just ask Tilya. She'll tell you all about it."

"Out!" Stacey said and pointed to the door. She rolled out of bed and rifled through the stack of albums leaning against the wall.

"Well, at least stop sulking," Linda Sue said. "You can go somewhere with me next time." She turned around to leave. "And by the way, something in your room smells to high heavens, like sour milk." She tilted her head to see an empty tub of ice cream with the Baskin Robbins logo on it not far from Stacey's foot, surrounded by dirty underwear.

Back in the kitchen, Linda Sue found Hetty squatting by the table.

"You okay?" she asked.

"Sure," she replied. "Just tired from all the packing."

⟐

July 18, 1976, 2:30 p.m.

Dear Diary,

No support from Lenny when I need it the most or from my oh-so-fantastic sisters. Would Lenny care if the knife block is chock-full of crumbs? Tilya probably doesn't know what a knife block is. Maybe she doesn't even own a knife. I'm completely exhausted. And depressed. I was packing the kitchen and suddenly I got the sense that I was crouching in the corner of the one room where we lived in the ghetto. Tilya and I were wrapped in each other's arms, watching two police officers enter and snatch him. A door slammed. Mama shrieked. He was gone.

Help! I've got to get away from these memories before they kill me. They're pulling me into a terrible darkness.

Always,
Hetty

Linda Sue

LINDA SUE AND JOSH arrived in Warsaw on a torrid day in August. Ace genealogists, they were not. Nobody would mistake these two anxious Americans for professional historians, archeologists, or photographers, although Josh was schlepping enough photography equipment to open a camera shop on Marszalkowska Street. They came with only a faint smattering of Berk lore because, as Linda Sue saw it, a conspiracy of silence had thwarted their efforts to unlock the family's past. They didn't have known addresses in Poland to investigate or land registries to consult.

"It's like looking for ghosts," Josh said to Linda Sue, his sculpted face gaunt with exhaustion as they waited on platform three of the Warsaw Central Railway Station for a train to Lodz. The intensity of the August heat had taken them by surprise. Dark semi-circles of sweat stained the armpits of Josh's button-down shirt. His damp black curls curved around the edge of his St. Louis Cardinals baseball cap. To their left, a blonde little girl in shorts and sandals sat on the top of her mother's upturned suitcase, propped up by the woman's fleshy knee. Just before the train was due to arrive, a platform change was announced. The crowd bustled from platform three to platform four, leaving Linda Sue and Josh scrambling to gather suitcases and backpacks in time to ascend the steep metal steps of the train.

The passageway through the second-class car was so narrow that Linda Sue and Josh had to squeeze past the other riders to find their reserved seats inside an assigned compartment. Linda Sue's clammy arm brushed against a strapping thirty-year-old. Six people were already sitting in their compartment. One, an elderly man closest to the door, was eating a roll and some sardines from a tin. Linda Sue stumbled over him to take her seat by the opened window.

"Sorry," she mumbled. Her English, she surmised from the blank look on his face, made no sense to him. His sidelong glance appeared to be a mixture of curiosity and suspicion occasioned by the unusual presence of foreigners on a train populated almost exclusively by Poles. Clutching her purse on her lap, Linda Sue gazed at the other passengers, briefly, without meeting their eyes. She wasn't sure why, but she got the feeling they knew that she and Josh were Jews. Something about the two of them must look Jewish here in Poland, she thought, more exotic than they looked in St. Louis or anywhere else she'd been in the USA. The train doors clicked shut. There was a jolt, and the train rattled out of Warsaw station. Linda Sue and Josh drifted off to sleep with the hot wind blowing and curtains billowing as they passed through the parched Polish countryside.

Their accommodation at the Grand Hotel in Lodz harkened back to the pre-war era by design, as if the intention had been to stop time. The marble lobby was perfectly preserved, full of ornate mirrors and traditional dark wood.

"Wow!" Linda Sue whispered to Josh, fidgeting with their luggage, too anxious to absorb the art deco elegance of the place. "Fabulous," she said.

"Does this hotel have flush toilets?" he asked. Beads of sweat dripped down his neck. "And air conditioning?"

"Yes and no," she said. "But what did you expect, Josh? Howard Johnson's?" She handed him a tissue to wipe away the driblets of perspiration collecting on his forehead. A small misgiving about travelling in Poland with Josh threatened to grow. Stop it, she said to herself, determined to carry on for her nephew's benefit. She threw back her shoulders, expanded her chest, and tipped her chin up. "This is a great location on one of the longest commercial streets in Europe. Let's dump our luggage and go for a walk." She promised him one of those Polish jelly donuts if he'd stop being such a *kvetch*.

They strolled along Piotrkowska Street—a hodgepodge of deteriorating tenements, booksellers, dress shops, bakeries, small grocery stores, restaurants, and cafés with a tram running down the street's midline. But Lodz, Linda Sue realized, was more than a city for her, and Poland was more than just a country. Here she and Josh were in this land that had once been home to the Berk family, yet there were no relatives left to greet them. Aunt Tzophia, her mother's sister, was not there to make her special *kasha varnishkes* for them. Their cousins Shana and Yitzy did not telephone to welcome them in Yiddish. The children of their cousins—children never born—were not chasing pigeons outside the Grand Hotel. She felt a sudden surge of homesickness. She desperately wanted to go home.

"Josh," she said while they dawdled in front of a window of glazed pastries.

"Yeah, Aunt Linda?" He pressed his nose to the glass.

"Nothing," Linda Sue said. "I just... I can't decide which pastry to choose."

"I'm getting the *paczki*," he said, entering the shop.

As they stood at the counter, surrounded by the smell of powdered sugar and receiving many surreptitious looks from the Polish customers, Linda Sue whispered, "I can't do this, Josh. I want to get away from here. I can call the guide and cancel for tomorrow."

"We just got here."

"So?"

"I'll never speak to you again." He scrunched his eyebrows

together in the same way that Hetty did when Linda Sue made her angry.

"Not a bad idea, Joshie." She poked him in the side and watched the plum jam from his *paczki* plop onto his running shoe.

✦

Linda Sue spotted him across the lobby as she descended the red carpeted stairs of the Grand Hotel. She watched him there, leaning against the warm Tuscan gold fireplace, and recalled how he had described himself on the phone the day before. "I'll be the ugliest guy around," he'd said. From a distance, he didn't strike her as particularly unattractive—there wasn't much competition at nine in the morning—nor did he match her notion of a guide. He was wearing jeans and a black t-shirt with his hair in a ponytail and a small cross suspended from his neck on a gold chain. A vest hung unfastened on his narrow frame.

"We're just waiting for my nephew Josh to finish breakfast," Linda Sue said when she introduced herself. "I hope you're not in a hurry."

Peter offered her a seat on the leather sofa nearby. "I belong to you all of today," he said. "Welcome to Woodzh. Please call me Peter. In Polish it's Piotr, but I know that's hard for Americans to say." With the palm of his hand, he smoothed his hair, fixing the silky strands that had come loose from an elastic band.

"Woodzh?" she blinked. "What's that?"

"That's the way Poles pronounce Lodz," Peter said. "If you ask someone in the Krakow train station who speaks English how to get to Lodz, they might send you to a ski lodge in the Tatra Mountains." He grinned. Before Linda Sue had a chance to react, Josh came striding through the lobby, his Leica bouncing on a strap over his shoulder, his shoelaces untied, and the fly of his pants mostly undone.

"Shall we begin?" Peter held the hotel door open for them

and nodded in the direction of the Baluty district and the Old Town where the ghetto had been. Along the way, he told them that the Germans had changed the name of Lodz to Litzmannsstadt, and sealed off the ghetto from the rest of the city in 1940 with barbed wire and wooden fences. The German security police had tightly guarded the enclosed area that consisted of 2,332 homes with 28,400 rooms. About 160,000 Jews had lived there with approximately seven people to a room. The data rushed from Peter in torrents, flooding Linda Sue and Josh with facts, numbers, dates, anecdotes, and historic photos selected from a binder that he carried under his arm. Linda Sue listened politely, but heard almost nothing he said. She looked into the dank stairwells of the desolate buildings they passed in Baluty, imaging Mama, Papa, Hetty, and baby Tilya living in a single room in one of these apartments. They had never mentioned that three other people might have been living with them. They never said who those people might have been.

"Hey, Peter," Josh interrupted when the abundance of details swamped him. "Like, how do you know all this stuff?"

"Don't be rude," Linda Sue said. "He's a teacher. In Lublin, right?" She had found Peter through her friend Fruma whose friend Rochelle had used Peter as a guide when her parents had returned to Lodz to visit a small textile factory that they had owned before the war. Or was it a mill? Linda Sue couldn't remember. "You will totally love this guy," Fruma had said to her. "Rochelle said he's really smart and charismatic. But..." She had pursed her lips in a half smirk.

"But what?" Linda Sue hated the way she always had to coax Fruma into divulging the most vital bits of information, the bits that made all previous information seem puny and irrelevant. "Just tell me," she had said to Fruma, expecting her to say Peter was married.

"He's not Jewish."

Now standing in front of a parish church at 8 Koscielna

Street, on the very spot where the epicentre of the Lodz ghetto had been, Linda Sue strained her head forward to give Peter more of her attention. The cross he was wearing gleamed in the sunlight. There wasn't a cloud anywhere for miles.

"This was the headquarters of the Kripo, the German criminal police," he said. "The 'Red House' it was called. Jews accused of smuggling or hiding valuable articles were tortured here."

"The Germans wore heavy black boots," Linda Sue added, closing her eyes. She remembered seeing her sisters imitate the march of the jackboots that they had heard as children in the hallway of their ghetto apartment: Hetty and Tilya straightening their skinny legs, clomping their feet, playing the Kripo game in the safety of U. City long after their confinement.

"Someone told you this?" Peter asked, noticing that Linda Sue was lost in remembrance.

"My sisters," she said.

Josh lifted his camera to photograph the parish church. The sun scorched its red bricks, as if to illuminate the building's brutal history. "I would have gotten out of this place as fast as I could. I would have ripped out the eyes of anyone who got in my way."

"Sorry. I understand how you feel, but you would have been caught instantly by a German guard," Peter said, "and publicly executed."

"Okay," Josh said, sounding skeptical for no good reason. Mounds of evidence had piled up proving the near impossibility of escaping from the Lodz ghetto. The Warsaw ghetto, maybe. But from the Lodz ghetto, escape had been virtually impossible.

"Can we take a lunch break?" Linda Sue asked. "And a camera break?" The constant click of Josh's Leica grated on her nerves. She had never intended their trip to Poland to be one long photo session. And there was something hostile in Josh's attitude toward Peter that bothered her; he seemed suspicious, unwilling to believe what Peter said. At every turn, Josh questioned him. She didn't need to be a mind reader to surmise what Josh was thinking: *Why was this non-Jewish Polish guy so immersed in every shred of Poland's Holocaust past?* Because that question had occurred to her, as well.

Peter recommended a milk bar for a cheap but wholesome lunch. He was quick to tell them that the state subsidized it. Linda Sue detected a hint of sarcasm in his voice, a cautious but critical tone.

"That's communism in Poland," Peter said. "Food shortages, long line-ups at the shops, and milk bars passing for restaurants." He glanced to see whether anyone was near them. The façade of the milk bar was nondescript, the interior simple and devoid of merriment. Not exactly the Golden Arches, Josh thought. A grim older woman who spoke no English took their order from Peter. Less than halfway into the meal, while Linda Sue was staring into her bowl of cold cherry soup, Josh stopped eating. He turned his Cardinals baseball cap backward with the bill resting on the back of his neck. The two top buttons of his shirt had come unfastened, exposing the hair on his chest matted with sweat. "So, Peter," he said. "Did you find our family in the list of Lodz ghetto residents? I guess my aunt Linda told you that our real name was Berkowitz. It was changed when our family came to America."

Peter took a gulp of watery juice and set the glass down on the table. He turned his neck until it cracked. "Yes, I do know that. And you might know that a registry was kept in the ghetto recording the names of all of the inhabitants by street address."

Linda Sue nodded. "Yeah, I tried to read everything I could find on the Lodz ghetto. I would never have imagined a statistical department operating in a ghetto. That's where Jewish photographers worked, taking pictures of the ghetto inmates for their identity cards."

"So you have heard of Mendel Grossman?" Peter said the name so softly they could hardly hear him. "He camouflaged his camera under his coat so he could take photos of how the Jews were forced to live."

"Yep. We know all about him," Josh said. "Aunt Linda gave me a book of his Lodz ghetto photos for my high school grad present. He was a totally awesome guy." A spontaneous smile crossed Josh's face as he touched his Leica resting on the chair next to him.

They waited for Peter to say something relevant to their family history. When he didn't say anything at all, Josh broke the uncertain silence. "Uh, what exactly can you tell us about the Berks or the Berkowitz family? That's, like, why we're here."

Linda Sue tapped Josh under the table with her foot. Why did this kid have to be so direct and aggressive—so all-American, all the time, particularly when Peter was being very nice to them? Maybe he was being *too* nice, she thought. Since when did Poles treat Jews nicely? She had read about the wave of violence and hostility directed at Jews returning to Poland after the war. Some Jews had been murdered in pogroms and others had found their property either occupied by non-Jewish Poles or expropriated by the communist government of Poland. All this niceness, she wanted to say to Peter, wasn't quite what the books had led her to expect. But she stopped herself. She glared at Josh.

"Be patient," she said.

"I understand," Peter replied. "Let me explain." Pulling the elastic band out of his hair, he lowered his voice a second time. "The records are now on microfilm here in Lodz, but they are very hard to use. Some records are missing or filed incorrectly. Entries are illegible. Names are duplicated or misspelled." His hair fell in disarray on his shoulders. Annoyed, he gathered all the flyaway strands into his palm and secured his hair with the band again.

"So how hard was it to find the name Berkowitz?" Josh asked.

Linda Sue added, more softly, "I thought the archives of the Lodz ghetto were supposed to be the most detailed records of any of Poland's ghettos."

"They are the most detailed," said Peter, "of the records that survived."

Linda Sue put down her spoon, pushed her soup bowl across the slick Formica table top, and stood up. The potato pierogi, which she'd compulsively eaten, too quickly, was a mistake. The whole thing sat like a glob in her gut.

"Where are you going, Aunt Linda?" Josh asked.

At the table near them, a prim woman, perhaps an office worker, sat with her head down and ate quietly. A bald man wearing a white short-sleeved shirt and drab pants ate alone at another. Nobody seemed to loiter in the milk bar. It wasn't that kind of place. Listening to the clatter of dirty plates accumulating at the self-serve window, Linda Sue had the urge to move on or run away.

Peter stood and touched her arm, beckoning her to sit down again. They sat down slowly. "I did find the names of your family in the list of Lodz ghetto residents," Peter said, "but not by the spelling you gave me." He pulled a folded sheet of paper from his vest pocket and showed them the Polish spelling of their name: Berkowicz.

"That's not our name," Josh said.

"It is," Peter gently insisted.

Josh glowered at him. "I should know our—"

"Look," Peter said. He tried to give Josh the sheet of paper. Instead, Linda Sue took it from Peter's hand. As she scanned the foreign words, Peter raised the complicated question of Jewish surnames which, he told them, were often recorded in Polish. Given names could also be tricky. There might have been dozens of diminutives, variants, and differences in spelling. Linda Sue examined the paper more closely. Her father's name, Simon, was spelled Szymon. Her mother's name

Hannah was Hana. Hetty, in America short for Henrietta, was listed as Yetta. Tilya was written as Zysla. Despite the muggy air in the milk bar, Linda Sue felt ice cold. Who were these people whose names seemed so strange to her? Was Berkowitz or Berkowicz even their real family name? And how many names could one family have in a lifetime? Peter rested his hand on her forearm. She was glad for his reassuring calm, which provided a bit of relief from the confusion in her head. She didn't want him to take his hand away, didn't want him to move it, not one inch.

In the list of given names supposedly belonging to the Berkowicz family, the third name down was the male name, Yeshua. Next to it, Peter had written a note: "Deported in 1942." Linda Sue slid the paper closer to Josh. "If these records are to be believed, there was a brother in our family named Yeshua. You are obviously named after him."

"A brother we never heard of?" Josh said. "Seriously, someone in the family would have told us that. Like Aunt Tilya. She isn't the type to lie."

"I'm not so sure about that, Josh," she said, stunned by the revelation. "Remember how all of them tried to protect us from being sad?" Her face looked pinched and ashen. The sound of her voice was shaky. She was becoming more restrained in the presence of Peter who, she feared, already knew too much about them. She decided to put an end to the conversation before it went any further. Peter said nothing. He glanced over his shoulder, watchful always.

As they were leaving the milk bar, Linda Sue vetoed their plan to visit the Jewish cemetery on Bracka Street. All of Poland was beginning to feel like a graveyard. Her ancestors seemed to have a hand on her ankle, pulling her underground with them. Peter proposed instead to conclude their tour at the Radegast train station, explaining that it was one of the most important landmarks in the history of the Litzmannstadt ghetto.

"I'm really not up for more touring today," Josh said. His otherwise bombastic tone had turned limp, more like a whimper. He shifted from one foot to another on the hot sidewalk while Peter quietly described the deliveries of fuel, food, raw materials, and manufactured goods that passed through the train station under the Nazis.

"It was the departure point for Jews being transported to the extermination camps at Chelmno and Auschwitz," Peter informed them. "And when Chaim Rumkowski—you know that he was the head of the Jewish Council of Elders—rounded up the children of the ghetto in 1942, they left from Radegast Station."

Peter's shoulders seemed less square as he spoke, his jawline softer. Looking at the purplish birthmark on the left side of his face, Linda Sue wasn't sure, but she thought she might be able to trust him, at least enough to go to the train station with him. But not one step further.

Josh resisted.

"Let me tell you how it happened," Peter said. "Maybe I am able to change your mind."

He told them how the Germans ordered the Jewish ghetto authorities to prepare twenty thousand people for deportation and how Rumkowski stood before the Jews of the Lodz ghetto and demanded that mothers and fathers give him their children. For eight days, a curfew kept Jews in their apartments while the German SS and police authorities, assisted by the Jewish ghetto police, went from building to building inspecting and selecting the elderly, the ill, and children under ten years old for deportation. Six thousand children were separated from their families and taken to Radegast Station.

Linda Sue grabbed Josh's hand. "You have to come with us."

Josh clenched his jaw. He didn't want to go, but he said, "Okay. I'm convinced."

Right before the taxi arrived to take them there, Josh

turned and snapped a picture of the milk bar. Years later, at an exhibit of his photography in San Francisco, Linda Sue would overhear a women ask her nephew why he had photographed that dingy little restaurant in Lodz. "Because that's where I began to understand the Holocaust," he would say. "Until then, it was just a fable."

❖

"Umschlagplatz." Peter said. "In German that means the collection point. The Umschlagplatz at Radegast Station was where inmates of the Lodz ghetto were brought under military escort for deportation directly to the Chelmno and Auschwitz extermination camps. This was the loading platform, the exact spot where the deportees gathered." The mid-afternoon sun cast shadows resting on other shadows. Peter opened his binder and flipped to the pages with grainy pictures of the Umschlagplatz as it was back then, teeming with deportees at the train doors, caps and scarves on their heads, holding bundles and suitcases, waiting for their departure.

Linda Sue took the binder and looked carefully at a photo of children, narrowing her eyes, searching their blurred faces. She didn't have an image of the boy she was looking for; she didn't know his age or size or the colour of his hair. She glanced at Josh, who was fiddling with his camera, and tried to remember him as a kid with dark curls and awkward limbs. She looked again at the photo, focusing on one boy with ringlets. Maybe that was him. She gripped the binder, lifting it closer to her eyes, as if to burn the image of that child into her memory.

Peter could feel her hands trembling. After a moment, with paternal gentleness, he took back the binder and shut it.

❖

August 6, 1976

Dear me,

I'm sitting on the ground at the Umschlagplatz at Radegast Station.

My only brother. Was he excited about the puffing of the engine? Did he hope to get a seat by the window, to look out at the fields and woods, small villages, winding brooks, cows in the pastures? Was he surprised when it wasn't a real train, but something like cars for transporting cattle? Was he frightened when the soldiers forced the old people, the people who were wheezing or limping, and the young children to climb into the cars? Was he holding someone's hand? Did someone help him up? Did he beg to be taken off the train when a Gestapo officer came to the window to check that the bars would not come loose? Did he cry when he heard the clatter of the iron doors sliding closed and the thick bolt click shut? Was he afraid of the soldiers sitting with bayonets on the train stairs? Did he gag as he watched two officers in long belted coats stroll down the length of the loading platform?

I once had a brother that Hetty and Tilya knew. How could they not have told me about him?

Goodbye, my only brother,
LS

Later, after they left Radegast Station, the three of them were standing together on Zielona Street, debating where to have dinner before Peter left them in Lodz to return to his hometown of Lublin. "I'm sorry," he apologized when there was no need for him to apologize. "Poland is a hard place for you. Good restaurants are not easy to find."

Linda Sue gazed at the windows on the third floor of an apartment building while they talked. She noticed an old woman's face half visible behind a curtain. Her gaze, observant as a hawk, seemed to pierce them with suspicion, assessing their Jewishness. Linda Sue rubbed her neck. She didn't typically consider herself delusional, but maybe she was learning to be paranoid in Poland. She had to remind herself that most Poles had never seen a Jew in their lives and would have no way of identifying her and Josh as Jewish unless... unless they were wearing horns or Star of David badges.

Peter followed Linda Sue's eyes. She felt an unexpected need to be taken care of by him. She didn't believe he could feel her vulnerability—no, he didn't and couldn't—but she hoped he might help her carry the burden of it.

"Would you and Josh like to come to Lublin with me?" he asked.

"Lubleeen?" Josh garbled the pronunciation. "It's not on the itinerary. And nobody I know has ever heard of that place." Linda Sue stifled a guffaw. His rock-solid rigidity was a Berk personality trait she easily recognized and tried unsuccessfully to control in herself.

Josh said, "If you want to go there, Aunt Linda, I'll meet you back in Warsaw."

"Fine by me," she said, by which she meant, *Are you nuts? What Berkowitz or Berkowicz or Berk by any other name would desert an eighteen-year-old American Jewish male in a communist country? What if he did something stupid and ended up in a Soviet gulag?*

"I'd like you to see my city," Peter said, interrupting Linda Sue's thoughts. He continued in a low voice. "And Majdanek. It was an extermination camp on the outskirts of Lublin. You might find it interesting. It was the first Nazi concentration camp to be liberated by the Allies in 1944."

"We're going to Auschwitz," Josh said. He felt Peter looking at him, about to say something more, but Josh folded his arms across his chest to show that he had made up his mind.

Linda Sue smiled at Peter. "You're kind. I would like to see Lublin and Majdanek even if Josh won't come with us. I'll take him back to Warsaw and meet you in Lublin."

"No, you go with Peter," Josh insisted. "I'm an adult, you know. I can take the train to Warsaw by myself."

"Are you sure you don't want to join us?" Peter said. "I'll rent a car if you would like and get a hotel room for both of you."

"I can't let you go back by yourself," Linda Sue said to Josh.

"I'm eighteen years old!" Josh replied. "Think about all the wild things I'd be doing as an eighteen-year-old back at home."

⬧

Rain had washed the sky a pewter gray by the time Linda Sue and Peter arrived at Majdanek the next day. They stepped off the trolley onto a busy main street four kilometres from the centre of Lublin and then walked the short distance to a massive stone monument which served as the gate to the former concentration camp. No trees surrounded the area to conceal the activities that had once occurred there, no river or forest to shield the concentration camp from view. There was nothing secretive about it, at this moment or before.

"You mean...." Linda Sue paused as she entered through the gate. "You mean, people passed by here every day? People could see everything?"

"It was originally a forced labour camp."

"For how long?"

"A few years."

"But then—"

"Yes, then it was turned into a death camp."

Linda Sue shook her head, as if refusing to believe the information. "And people knew that?" she asked.

"They must have," Peter said, looking at the crematorium's smoke stack and the building with the gas chamber. "They knew something, but maybe they didn't ask too many questions."

On a large field of grass close to the street stood a white stucco farmhouse. "That's where the camp commandant lived with his family," Peter said.

"The family lived on the premises of a death camp? I don't believe it." Linda Sue gave another incredulous shake of her head. "Did his wife ask him over dinner how his day went? Did she say, 'Please pass the cabbage rolls, honey. How many Jews did you gas today?'"

Peter didn't answer. A fine, mist-like rain prickled their faces.

It was late in the afternoon and the Majdanek museum was closed, but they were still allowed to roam the concentration camp grounds. Barely covered by Peter's umbrella, they headed toward the wooden barracks that had housed the inmates. Inside were rows of cages stuffed with the victims' shoes tied together in pairs. They were mostly men's gray lace-ups, but there were a few women's shoes made of red leather, and some infants' boots, creased, with scuffed toes. Bunk beds were stacked three high.

"Every morning the girls in these bunks had to line up outside to be counted," Peter said. "One morning a girl of about twelve or thirteen felt sick and refused to go to the roll call. Blood ran down her legs, and she assumed she was dying. The other girls knew she would be killed if she didn't come out of the barracks so they scrubbed her clean and propped her up in the yard. Later in the evening, they quietly celebrated her becoming a woman."

"That's a great story," Linda Sue said.

"Yes, her body continued to work even though the Nazis considered her to be sub-human."

"So did this young woman survive?"

"I don't know."

"Yeah, well, my sister didn't survive."

"Which one? Zysla?"

"No," she replied. "No, I had a third sister, who died when she was seventeen in the States."

"I'm sorry," Peter said.

"For what?" She looked at him briefly, then looked away.

As they trudged further along the path, a sudden summer hailstorm pelted them with stones. Peter pulled her into the nearest building. What she saw first were containers of Zyklone B poisonous gas. Dizzy, Linda Sue reached out to him. She felt herself buckling. He set her down by the nearest gas chamber wall to comfort her. "Are you okay?"

Their eyes met for a second, but they didn't speak. Peter

allowed her to have that silence. After a few minutes, she said, "Not okay."

But she forced herself to stand, to continue. They walked along the same road toward the mausoleum.

"Here," Peter said, pulling Linda Sue gently toward him under the umbrella. She tensed. "Just so you don't get drenched by the rain."

The mausoleum looked like a massive stone bowl set on a hill above the concentration camp. In it were the ashes of hundreds of cremated Jews, mixed with a few bones and cement to prevent the ashes from blowing away. Someone had left a candle in a small tin can at the base of the mausoleum.

"Do you have a match?" Linda Sue asked Peter. He jammed his fingers into his jeans pocket to find his lighter, knelt down, and cupped the tin can in his hand. He lit the candle while she said the first line of the Mourner's Kaddish: "Yit'gadal v'yit'kadash she'mei raba." Unfamiliar with the Jewish prayer, Peter kept still. He tucked the burning candle into the corner of the mausoleum steps to protect it from the rain. And to hide it.

"My grandparents on my father's side were Jewish."

"Really? Don't take this personally, but you don't look Jewish."

"My mother is one-hundred percent Polish Catholic," he said.

"What about your dad? Does he do Shabbat or anything?"

"My father? He's not a bit religious. I'd say he is one-hundred percent secular." Peter stuck his hand into the air to determine whether the rain had stopped.

"Well, maybe he isn't religious because it hasn't been safe to be Jewish here," she said.

"Maybe. We never talk about what happened."

"Neither do we," she said, watching him lower the umbrella. She gulped, trying to hold back tears, and started to turn away. He touched her arm, his fingers lingering there for a few seconds, pulsing on her skin, long enough for Linda Sue to register the warmth of his touch.

That evening, pressed against his lithe body in a narrow hotel bed, she listened to the roosting pigeons coo under the eaves while Peter spoke in a whisper about his Jewish grandparents. She caught his silvery blue eyes staring at the ceiling. His body had a distinctive scent, a little like musty wood. She flared her nostrils and sniffed. The smell didn't nauseate her; it didn't alarm her. She simply took it in.

"I was told never to mention our Jewish background to anyone. It didn't exist," he said, caressing her nipple over and over with his thumb. He placed his leg on top of her thigh and propped himself up on an elbow. "Do you care if I smoke?"

Linda Sue didn't care if Peter smoked. She didn't care if his grandparents had converted to Christianity before the war to avoid antisemitism and had kept their Jewish heritage a secret. She didn't care if he looked as Polish as the Hollywood actress Kim Novak who had starred in Linda Sue's favourite Hitchcock film, *Vertigo*. She didn't care that he was baptized Catholic and knew nothing about Jewish traditions or prayers, not even the Mourner's Kaddish. None of these things mattered in the least to her. But his mother was Polish Catholic, and that fact could never be changed. Nor had he been circumcised at birth. In her father's eyes, in the eyes of the religion, Peter was not Jewish. He lacked the essential proof. For Papa, the Polish people were so mired in the Holocaust that he would always regard Peter with a heavy dose of suspicion. Long before any family discussion of that sort occurred and well before a future with Peter was even broached—the mere idea of it seemed absurd and awful and oh-so-wonderful all at the same time—she knew that Papa would not accept Peter's quiet embrace of a Jewishness that wasn't really his to claim.

Linda Sue slipped off the bed and went to think in the bathroom. She had agreed to stay over in Lublin one night, but no longer. Any more time away from Josh would only sink her further into a pit of Jewish guilt so ever present that she hardly noticed it. She bit her lower lip. She imagined Papa dying of a heart attack when his youngest daughter announced one Shabbat that she was moving to Poland. She heard the thumping of his heart stop dead. She remembered his never-ending wish for more Jewish grandchildren. As she rinsed her hands, her eyes fixed on a crack in the porcelain sink. She flinched, telling herself it was somehow a bad omen. Besides, she could never learn to speak Polish. She had tried, but even her attempts to pronounce Peter's name in Polish always ended in an embarrassing failure.

"I'm leaving on the first train to Warsaw tomorrow," Linda Sue announced on her return from the bathroom. She slipped into bed and curled into his waiting arm.

"Will I ever see you again?" he asked.

"I don't know. Do you want to?"

"Do you?"

"I bet you sleep with all the American tourists you guide," she said.

"What makes you think that?"

"Do you?"

"Will you write me when you get home?" he asked evasively.

"Yes, if you write me first."

He drifted off to sleep. She lay awake, listening to him breathing, feeling the steady rise and fall of his body next to hers. Scenarios played in her head. She imagined the life she would lead with him, but her breath quickened each time she tried to enter one of the scenes.

"I—I can't see our future together," Linda Sue said when she kissed him goodbye in the morning.

✦

Eight days later, Linda Sue and Josh watched their luggage disappear on the airport conveyor belt. They were more disconnected than connected after weeks of travel together in Poland. More knowledgeable, for sure, but also more confused. Perhaps they had gained wisdom, but with it came grief. Linda Sue bought Josh a treat as they walked to their gate. That was her last-ditch effort to make amends. She refused to stoop any lower to compensate for whatever was bothering him which, she surmised, was not about her abandoning him in Lodz. That separation had been liberating and necessary for both of them. She supposed he was angry—and every Berk would be angry—that she had slept with Peter, a Pole no less. But she felt obliged to level with Josh about what had happened with Peter.

"So?" Linda Sue said to Josh, waving a raspberry-filled chocolate bar in his direction. He continued to mope. She admitted that the last half of the trip had been challenging. Several days roaming around the Old Town in Krakow had lifted their spirits, but a side trip from Krakow to Auschwitz had dazed them into silence. On the bus ride back, Linda Sue had suggested a couple of days in the mountainous resort town of Zakopane for a change in scenery. She told Josh that Bubbie had adored Zakopane as a child. Josh didn't believe her. The Bubbie he knew, the one who made him chicken soup if he so much as sneezed and sometimes spent the afternoon in her nightgown, would never have placed a baby toe on the Carpathian mountain chain. Josh suspected, however, that Peter hiked there on a regular basis and had recommended it highly. Nevertheless, Josh agreed to a short stay in Zakopane before they returned to Warsaw for their departure.

"Well," Linda Sue said to Josh while they waited for their flight. "How do you feel about our trip?"

Josh shrugged. He took several bites of the chocolate bar, chewing every morsel as if he were tasting Wedel chocolate for the very first time when, in fact, he had been sampling the various offerings of the famous Polish chocolate maker daily, often hourly. He said to his aunt, "It feels like we've come all this way without finding what we were looking for."

"You sound disappointed."

Josh stared at his chocolate-covered fingers. "Disappointed? That's one way to look at it." His Leica, the only carry-on item he had, was pressed against his chest. "We still don't know how the four of them managed to stay alive in the Lodz ghetto. We think they were there until the end. We think they lost a son by the name of Yeshua, but we can't prove any of this."

After a minute, Linda Sue replied, "We're not their lawyers, you know. We don't have to prove anything to anyone."

"I guess I wanted more evidence of something. I'm not sure what I was looking for, but after you took off with Peter..." The corners of Josh's mouth tugged downward. He looked away. "I didn't go directly back to Warsaw, you know. I stayed in Lodz to visit the Jewish cemetery."

Linda Sue tilted her head back. "I don't get it. You weren't keen for Peter to take us there."

"So I changed my mind. Big deal. I'm allowed to change my mind." He wiped his hands on the side of his pants.

"It's just that Peter would have been happy to take you to the Jewish cemetery." She looked at Josh's lips, which were as straight and thin as a pencil, with traces of candy at both ends.

"Maybe I wanted to see it by myself, without you and your new boyfriend. I wanted to see for myself why Mendel Grossman had spent so much time at the cemetery. And..."

"And what?"

"And I wanted to find a Berkowitz tombstone or something, anything tangible that would have connected me to them."

"Honestly, Josh. Peter would have been the best guide for that."

He glowered at her. "No problem. The hotel found me a guide, an older man named Andrzejek. A retired school teacher." He wiped the chocolate from his lips. "Not your type, Aunt Linda. Anyway, it was raining when we got there."

"Yep, it was raining at Majdanek, too." She felt a shiver in her body, recalling the way Peter had touched her. "So did you find anything about the Berkowitz family at the cemetery?"

"I did," Josh said, to Linda Sue's surprise. "Did you know—"

"Wait," Linda Sue said.

She found different seats for them near the terminal windows, where other passengers would not be privy to any discoveries Josh made in the Jewish cemetery. "Did you know that dead bodies from the ghetto arrived at the cemetery on carts every day, Aunt Linda?" he said, glancing around for possible spies. "Mendel Grossman managed to photograph the faces of the dead before the gravediggers buried them in a mass grave. Can you imagine doing that? Photographing dead people? And their faces, bruised and crushed and bloody, some with eyes closed, others with eyes half opened. Adults and children. He put a number on their chests so that someday they could be matched with his photos and identified by their families."

"Did your guide tell you that?"

"No, I read it in that book you gave me about Mendel Grossman. Remember? It said—" The boarding announcement cut their conversation short.

Once they were settled on the plane, Linda Sue turned to Josh. "I want to know more about the cemetery."

"Later," he said. "Once I get my photos developed." He held his Leica on his lap for take-off.

◆

August 15, 1976

Dear me,

First Shabbat since we've been back. Very low key. Josh and I only shared the sanitized version of our trip and a few photos of Piotrkowska Street that I snapped with my dinky camera. Hetty and Papa looked. They nodded, but made no comment. (Lenny and Stacey were barely paying attention.) I took from this, rightly or maybe wrongly, that whatever happened to them in Poland was going to stay in Poland. Seeing Papa and Hetty hold the pictures in their hands like strangers, I sort of understood. It was such a long time ago, and I'm not sure they still remember many of the details. Or they don't want to remember. Or they prefer to forget. Or they forgot to remember. Or they remembered to forget. Whatever.

Josh and I haven't really talked about Yeshua or Peter. And I haven't said a thing to Tilya about what happened in Poland either. Why should I? She knew about Yeshua and refused to tell me when I specifically asked her about our family secrets. I'm crushed. Devastated. Furious with her. I expected so much more from Tilya, the ruthlessly honest, fearless Berk.

But I did have a dream which made me feel a little better. Right in the middle of it, my friend Fruma suddenly said, "Hey, Linda Sue, you're dreaming right now, so you can say whatever you want to your Polish boyfriend." Everything seemed to slow down and become incredibly vivid and real, even though I knew I was dreaming. So I said, "I love you, Piotr. I wish I could have stayed."

Toodle-oo for now,
LS.

Hetty

HETTY CHECKED THE FRIDGE one last time. It was their final Sunday morning in the old house on Stanford. A pint of chocolate milk and a quarter of a block of Philadelphia cream cheese were all that remained on the crusty fridge shelves. She decided to chuck them both, disposing of the milk down the sink and too much of the cream cheese straight down her throat. She left the kitchen full of remorse, but stopped when she reached the staircase. She had forgotten to clean out the freezer. *Frozen veggies would hardly be an appropriate gift for the new homeowners, now would they?* She laughed. Someone had eaten most of the bag of Green Giant Summer Sweet Peas. Curious, she asked Josh about the missing peas when she was doing the final sweep of his room.

"Yeah, I ate them last night. Unthawed."

"You couldn't boil them?"

"Uh..." He noticed his mother's gaze hoovering his bookshelves, desktop, and the ripped seat of his swivel chair for any debris that hadn't been discarded yet. The surfaces appeared pristine, more junk-free and dustless than in all the years of his boyhood.

"What's with those envelopes on the bed?" she asked.

"Nothing."

"Nothing?"

"Nothing."

"How could they be nothing?

"They just are nothing." He walked over to the bed and scooped up the half dozen envelopes containing the photos of the Poland trip—images of the Lodz ghetto where his mother had been a terrified child, the Umschlagplatz at Radegast Station where his namesake Yeshua had vanished, the Jewish cemetery where his grandfather had dug the trench that might have been his own grave. All those photos had captured something in Josh—his voyage of discovery, his transformation from a sheltered U. City kid to a young man on the cusp of adulthood.

"You know, you never showed us any of the pictures you took in Poland," Hetty said. We only saw some snapshots that Linda Sue took. They weren't very interesting."

He buried all six envelopes in his knapsack. "You know... you're right."

⁂

September 5, 1976, 11:35 p.m.

Dear Diary,

Wonder of wonders. We've arrived in Frontenac! Even the air smells fresher out here. Boxes everywhere. It will take me months to put this house in shape. By myself, needless to say. I feel so alone most of the time that I sometimes wish I wasn't alive. Stacey starts at her new high school right after Labour Day. And Josh, well... He just doesn't seem like the same sweet boy I raised. All my hard work—my blood, sweat, and tears! I knew he and Linda Sue should never have gone to Poland. G-d only knows what they discovered over there. Neither one is talking. Maybe it really is better that he is leaving for the University of Michigan tomorrow if you know what I mean.

To be continued.

Always,
Hetty

Linda Sue

L INDA SUE STARTED THE NEW school term feeling despondent. The bustle of September usually energized her, but not this year. She felt uncommunicative, almost anti-social when a gaggle of fifth graders rushed into her classroom for the first time. It was so unlike her. How would she be able to inspire a joy in learning when she felt like such a killjoy? It was all Josh's fault, she grumbled. His departure for university added one more name to her list of losses, though she and Josh weren't separated by anything insurmountable, like death, or an ocean or religion.

After school, she dragged herself home, flipped on the radio and slid her feet into her house slippers. The barrage of news about the presidential election only annoyed her further. She refused to discount Jimmy Carter as presidential material on the grounds that he was a relatively unknown peanut farmer. She personally had nothing against peanuts—which, she knew, were a good source of protein—nor did she have anything against Washington outsiders which, she knew, couldn't be worse than the insiders who gave Americans Watergate and Vietnam. Thank you very much. She was about to smash the radio against the wall. No, she decided instead to conduct a search for the best earplugs available to create artificial deafness until the last vote was counted in November. Suddenly the phone rang, interrupting her diatribe.

"Hey, Aunt Linda!" Josh sounded upbeat on the other end of the line.

"I was just thinking about you, kiddo."

"Really?"

"Yeah, really. How's it going up there in Ann Arbor?"

"Not bad, not bad."

"So how are your courses?"

"Uh... fine, fine."

"Just fine?"

"What's wrong with fine?"

"Nothing's wrong with fine. So which courses are fine?"

"I've only been to a couple of classes, but Western Civ seems pretty interesting."

"Don't tell me Western Civ is still being taught. I thought they decommissioned that old battleship years ago."

"Look, I didn't call to talk about the university curriculum. I want to know if my mom told you about the little scuffle we had before I left."

"No. Should she have?"

"She didn't tell you about our discussion of my photos?"

"Which photos?"

"The photos I took in Poland. You were with me. Sort of. Sometimes."

"Oh, *those* photos.

"I never showed them to my mom, and now she's angry at me."

"And?"

"And don't you think that's completely unfair?" A sense of outrage was beginning to build in his voice.

"Unfair? How is it unfair?"

"C'mon. She's withheld every speck of information about Poland from me. She didn't tell me I'm named after her dead brother. She let us go to Poland without a glimmer of the facts, and now she expects me to tell her what really happened in six packages of glossy Kodak prints. How is that fair?"

"I agree. It's not fair, but..."

"But what?"

"But, did anyone ever tell you life's not always about what's fair?" Linda Sue asked. "They're amazing photos, Josh. You should do something with them. Maybe you can use them in Western Civ."

"Sorry. It doesn't work like that."

"Sure it does. What do you think your Western Civ course is about? Bupkis? It's about the rise and fall of European civilization."

"So?"

"So you stood on the spot where the fall became self-evident, not one but lots of those depraved spots. You documented them with your camera."

"I did, didn't I..." Josh paused. "By the way, did I tell you I might change my first name to Jeremy?"

"And crush Zaidie like Tilya did?"

"I said I'm *considering* it. I haven't done it yet."

By the time Josh was ready to graduate from the University of Michigan, he was still Josh. He was Josh when he got married, became a father, and travelled to Israel to exhibit his photos, a body of work that had taken shape in his fourth year at the university when he earned a coveted place in the senior seminar on modern Europe. As the culminating project in that class, he submitted a photo essay titled "Time, Mortality, and Sacred Places of Remembering."

The eight students in Josh's seminar and his professor, the preeminent social historian, Charles Tilly, heard the tremor in Josh's voice when he read the essay aloud late one afternoon in May. A stillness settled on the dimly lit room. The full collection of his photos from the Jewish cemetery in Lodz continued to spool, projected on a screen behind him. It was the first time the collection was viewed in its entirety. Josh would always credit Professor Tilly for encouraging him to become either an historian or a photographer. Josh thought that meant he should do both. Among the notebooks and stacks of file folders eventually found in Hetty's basement, there was a handwritten copy of "Time, Mortality, and Sacred Places of Remembering." No one in the family had ever bothered to read it.

❖

September 11, 1976

Dear me,

Nothing good on television tonight. I've been back from Poland about a month, but I haven't heard from Peter yet. Don't know what I'm feeling. Something between horribly let down and miserable regret. Can't really talk to my sisters about him. It's too complicated. But honestly, what can I talk to my sisters about? At least Josh might be able to salvage something useful from our trip to Poland. Early to bed.

Toodle-oo for now,
LS.

Part III

Baby Steps

1980–1981

Toni

EARLY ONE MORNING in February, Toni lay in bed trying to prolong the moment when her day would officially begin. Daylight poured through the narrow window in her bedroom, startling her with its intensity and abundance. For a moment, she wondered if she were in St. Louis rather than in New York on the fifth floor of a walk-up with a claw-foot bathtub in the kitchen. At least her tiny tenement on East 27th Street was closer to the college than her old apartment uptown. Most of the time, a subway ride wasn't necessary. She could walk the distance in nineteen brisk minutes, and, on a clear day with no memories jangling her mind, she could observe the Empire State building from her bedroom window.

Toni felt Galaxy's chocolate-coloured paws graze her face and the cat's forehead butting against her cheek. She groaned, but the cat ignored her and continued to rub against her skin until Toni's mouth was full of creamy white cat hair.

"What *chutzpah*," she said. Not a trace of anger was evident in Toni's voice. She was one of those people who preferred pets to humans most of the time. She coddled her Siamese cat like it was an abandoned child, smothering the animal in unconditional love. She would gladly empty her bank account to pay the vet bills if the cat vomited more than twice in a week. X-rays, bloodwork, electrocardiograms. Toni smiled at Galaxy while picking strands of baby-fine feline hair off her lips. "Well, you do have the most beautiful blue eyes," she said. "Shaped just like almonds. You know that?" The cat purred, satisfying Toni's hunch that it understood every word. "I need to dress you in funny hats, Galaxy," Toni scratched the cat's arched back. "Like the pictures of the cats Hetty used to draw for me in the ghetto. We never saw a real cat there. What cat could stay alive in that cesspool of filth? We hardly managed to survive."

The ring of the phone interrupted their playtime. When Toni finally lifted the receiver to her ear, she heard Marion Thomas say hello in that northern Louisiana drawl of hers, unmistakable now that they had become close friends.

"Marion, why are you calling me at this ungodly hour?" Toni asked. She pushed Galaxy off her mattress which sat on the floor. She didn't have a box spring. The double bed extended almost to the outer walls of the room. She had to walk (or crawl) across the mattress every time the phone rang. "Where are you, anyway?"

"St. Louis. Where do you think?" Marion sounded hurt that Toni seemed to have forgotten she was teaching part-time in the anthropology department at Wash U., her first job after defending her dissertation on young Black kids growing up in Pruitt–Igoe. "I've got a mind to hang up on you," she said. "You and your disremembering."

"Very funny," Toni said and without thinking added, "Runs in the family." Her eyes panned the room for her notes on Kate Millett's *Sexual Politics*, which she had last seen on the pillow where Galaxy slept. "Sorry, I'm feeling distracted. So, what's on your agenda at this early hour? I've got an eight o'clock class, but my lecture notes seem to have gone missing."

"Oh, just wing it. You don't need notes anyway. I'm teaching today, too. Ethnography 101," Marion said. "But I've got to talk to you."

"You mean about the women's movement or what?"

"Yeah, about the women's movement and race and how

the two intersect. Can't you see? We're cutting ourselves off from Black women! And nobody cares two hoots about what happened to all those residents from Pruitt–Igoe."

"Well, I do care," Toni said. "That's not the problem."

"You care, right. But you haven't experienced racism in the way we have, not to mention being poor or..."

"Slow down for a minute. Can we talk about this at a better time?"

"Okay," Marion said. "I just thought..."

"I'll be in St. Louis before I go to the rally in Chicago. We can talk then."

"Catch you later," Marion said abruptly and hung up. Toni walked into the kitchen to clear last night's teacups off the rectangular piece of plywood that served both as a lid for the bathtub and her makeshift table. The tips of the leaves on her hanging spider plant had turned brown, its tendrils pushing out of the soil like fingers searching for something to grasp. Toni noticed but didn't have time to water it. Instead, she fastened the plywood onto hooks above the bathtub, turned on the taps, and swung her left leg over the side for a quick sponge bath before class.

⫶

Toni and her feminist colleagues had the smarts to organize a rally. And the know-how. Hell, they had participated in dozens of demonstrations across the country in the years following the passage of the Equal Rights Amendment by Congress. That was in 1972, and here they were, almost eight years later, without ratification of the ERA by the required thirty-eight states. Totally gross, Toni raged. *How revolutionary was it to guarantee women the same rights as men?* Unbelievable. That was the word that best described her frustration with the whole fiasco.

Of course, Toni supported the National Organization of Women's demonstration in Chicago scheduled for Mother's Day. She had marched with the New York City chapter of

NOW in their Walk Against Rape in Central Park. She had applauded NOW for its stand against the Tiffany's ad—the one that stated the three most important decisions a woman would make in her lifetime concerned her crystal, her silver pattern, and her china. What a joke that was. She had participated in Shirley Chisholm's run for the Democratic nomination for president and still treasured her stash of "Shirley Chisholm for President" buttons. The urgency of the NOW Mother's Day march in Chicago wasn't lost on Toni. Illinois must, it absolutely must, ratify the ERA amendment—do or die. Representatives from every state in the union and delegations from over three hundred organizations were going to attend. All of Toni's feminist colleagues would be there. The first woman mayor of Chicago was going to address the rally, and Jesse Jackson had promised to make an appearance. She planned to carry a placard stating in bold block letters, *WOMEN WEREN'T BORN DEMOCRATS, REPUBLICANS, OR YESTERDAY.*

On the morning of the Chicago demonstration, Toni was in St. Louis at Linda Sue's house, eager to catch an early train north. In addition to her placard, she was carrying enough almonds and raisins to feed an army of unstoppable women. She made a quick detour to see Papa before she departed for the station.

Toni touched her father's skin, yellowish and papery with old age. She looked at him in bed, gazing into his half-closed eyes behind his glasses held together with epoxy glue. They were sad eyes that made her want to repair the past for him, as if the whole universe were just like her lecture hall, and she could control everything in it. Maybe she should adopt a baby in Poland, Toni thought. To make him happy. Papa kept hold of her hand. Her head felt muddled. She was vaguely aware of her surroundings. She was in Papa's bedroom. She was sitting next to him on the bed. A few books were stacked on the table beside him. A spring breeze stirred the trees outside his window. But the air felt so thick that her head ached. When Papa gave her a wan smile and another tug on her hand, she couldn't respond. She closed her eyes. For an instant, she was back in Lodz, cowering in the corner of their apartment in the ghetto with Hetty. Papa and Mama were whispering something to Yeshua on the other side of the room. She saw them combing their hands through his hair, kissing his forehead.

"Yeshua." Toni heard his name unintentionally slip from her lips.

"If he were buried six feet deep under the ground, I bet you would still know your brother," Papa said.

Toni lifted her eyes to Papa. She blinked. The sound of his slow, uneven breathing held her there. She couldn't leave him, not even to attend such an important march in Chicago with her devoted colleagues, her chosen sisters.

⬥

May 11, 1980

Mama always said, "You can never miss a train."

Really? I just did, and I've never felt so disloyal and split into a million tiny pieces in my life. There's no way that I could abandon my father, but I need my friends, too. At least they understand and support who I am.

Sisterhood is powerful,
Toni

Linda Sue

"WHAT DO YOU MEAN she's not available?" The woman on the phone sounded indignant. "She never mentioned she would be leaving St. Louis in such a hurry."

"Who's calling?" Linda Sue asked. She didn't recognize the voice, but the lethal combo of impatience and importance sounded all too familiar. It reminded her of Tilya when she wanted to let you know she had no time to waste on small talk. Because, as her sister never failed to remind her, the fate of women everywhere could only be improved through active organizing and tackling the interlocking issues of gender, race, sexuality, and class. Anything else wasn't worth her breath.

"It's Marion Thomas, a colleague of Toni's."

"Yes," Linda Sue said.

"Just wondering why Toni was in such a hurry to get out of town. Is anything wrong?"

"I'm sorry. She didn't give us reasons, never does really." Over the years, Tilya had become so reserved about her private life that the family had stopped asking. Marion Thomas sounded skeptical, as if Linda Sue were withholding information when, in fact, she was simply the messenger who happened to be visiting Papa on her way home from teaching when the phone rang. She had hesitated to answer, but then it rang again and again, sounding increasingly desperate. After three calls of twenty-two rings each within a ten-minute timespan, Linda Sue had succumbed.

"I really don't believe it," Marion Thomas said.

"I hate to disappoint you," Linda Sue replied. Only after she spoke did she remind herself that *she* wasn't the one who'd disappointed this woman. *She* didn't flee St. Louis without explanation. She was firmly planted right here.

"Well, can you at least tell me why Toni didn't come to the march in Chicago? Did something happen?"

"Nothing happened that I know of," Linda Sue said, glancing over at Papa sitting on the sofa with his crocheted shawl around his shoulders despite the balmy spring weather. For the past year, he'd been wearing long underwear in the heat of summer and drinking scalding tea even when the thermometer registered 102 degrees in the house. The newspaper he was reading had fallen onto the floor when he dozed off.

She did a quick recall of the previous day, a complicated Sunday, to be sure, because the Berks never celebrated Mother's Day, not even when Mama was alive. Papa and Mama said it was too *goyish*, too American. A likely excuse. It was what they always said to hide their feelings, which Linda Sue suspected had more to do with the cruel loss of their own mothers than the rejection of true-blue Americana, whatever that was.

Tilya also shunned Mother's Day, but on entirely different grounds. *Hogwash* was the term she most typically used to describe the commercialization of motherhood. As far as she was concerned, it was a capitalist scheme to increase the sale of roses and carnations. And if she had her way, all mothers of the world would unite on the second Sunday in May and wear t-shirts that read *No time for patriarchy!*

"You know, we were all waiting for her at the rally," Marion Thomas said.

Linda Sue wasn't listening. She was still stuck on their complicated Mother's Day. Looking back, she thought Hetty had seemed particularly agitated yesterday. Her marriage was deteriorating, and the children were slipping away from her. For a distraction, Hetty had lined up several clients to show them big homes with hammocks hanging between trees in shady spots at the back of the gardens. Throughout lunch, Hetty had constantly checked her watch to see if it was time for her appointments yet.

Tilya was in no better shape. She disliked the Branding Iron, the popular ranch style restaurant that Hetty had chosen for their Mother's Day lunch.

"Who would use the name *branding iron* for a restaurant?" Tilya had said when they took their seats. "I feel like we're at a cattle or slave auction. It's enough to wreck my appetite."

"Lighten up, Tilya. Can't you turn off your politics for once in your life and be normal?" Hetty had asked.

At the ginger-coloured pine table next to them, Kimberly Kellerman, an old acquaintance of theirs from U. City High, had gathered her three teenage kids, her husband (presumably her first, but who knew anymore), and an elderly couple that looked like grandparents. Three generations. A full deck. A dream the Berk sisters feared they would never achieve.

Tilya had clenched her jaw at the sight of them and turned her head away to avoid making direct eye contact with Kimberly Kellerman.

"Are you at least going to say hello?" Hetty had pressed Tilya.

"No, you say hello. I hardly remember Kimberly Kellerman," Tilya had whispered. "Maybe we were in an English class together. For one semester at most." Tilya had glanced at their table and given a reluctant nod of recognition. Her eyes nervously skimmed the faces of Kimberly Kellerman's handsome children, as though a ticking time bomb had landed in her lap.

"Sorry, Marion, that I can't be of more help. I'll let Tilya know that you called," Linda Sue said returning to the present.

"Who's Tilya?" Marion Thomas asked.

"Oh, that's our pet name for Toni. Don't tell her I told you. Bye for now." Linda Sue started to put the receiver down.

"Wait! Just one minute more, if you don't mind. Do you live in St. Louis?" Marion Thomas asked with an assertiveness that reminded Linda Sue of the first time she had seen her on television.

"I do," said Linda Sue. "For my whole life."

"Then listen up. You might be interested in what we are trying to do in this city." Marion Thomas paused for effect. "Just because we were told to be quiet as children doesn't mean we have to accept the threat of sexual abuse, poverty, and racism for the rest of our lives."

"Uh... thank you for calling," Linda Sue stammered. She looked across the room at Papa still sleeping. She remembered when the family watched the destruction of Pruitt–Igoe together. He had been on his feet with Josh, attentive and so much stronger.

May 12, 1980

Dear me,

I had the weirdest telephone call of my life while I was checking on Papa after school today. The caller had a kind of southern accent and introduced herself as Marion Thomas, a friend of Tilya's. Wow! She's one forceful lady. And a million times more interesting than we are. I imagine Tilya and Marion Thomas having fabulous conversations about how to liberate women while Hetty and I sit around worrying about whether Papa will take his next breath and what we will have for Shabbat dinner. To be perfectly honest, I'm hugely jealous of Marion's power. She would have no problem following her destiny. She would have moved to Poland if she wanted to, married Peter, and had six kids without looking back.

She would have learned Polish and made pierogies while staying true to herself and her values. Next to her, I feel like a big wimp.

Toodle-oo for now,
LS.

Hetty

HETTY WASN'T HOME. Stacey sat alone on the cushioned window seat gazing at their untended backyard in Frontenac. The ominous clouds from earlier that morning were gone, and the sky was a bright, vacant blue. Sometimes she was lucky enough to spot a white-tailed deer grazing out there. At night, the occasional howl of a coyote interrupted the stillness. Once or twice, a coyote even appeared at the garden's edge. She saw it skulking behind her mother's rhododendrons and heard its strange yip-yapping. The worst was the time when she pulled into the driveway and confronted a pair of eyes shining in the glare of the car's headlights. She sat behind the steering wheel trembling until her mother came home and rescued her. Remembering that scary incident, Stacey twisted her face in displeasure and headed for the kitchen.

She went directly to the fridge. She opened it and peered in, swinging the door back and forth with her arm. She was having a craving, but found nothing that satisfied her. Why in this perfect kitchen, she railed, did her mother leave nothing decent to eat? Like a pint of Baskin-Robbins chocolate mint ice cream, which she had sampled on one of those cute miniature pink spoons after school the other day. At least her mother could make cookies, like her friends' mothers. How hard was that? Her dad had never seemed thrilled with the move to this humongous house. He had left a couple of years after the family pulled up stakes in U. City and settled in Frontenac. Josh didn't return after he graduated from university, but no one had really expected him to come back home. She shut the fridge door and progressed from the kitchen through the panelled den. The craving for something good to eat was still there—it was always there—but she decided that it wasn't a craving for food. No, it was a craving to do something or have an awesome experience or... she didn't know what.

As Stacey made her way down the long hall to her bedroom, she caught a glimpse of the family photos lined up like train cars, one after another, covering the wall: Josh's Bar Mitzvah, herself and Josh romping on a beach in Florida, Aunt Tilya holding her doctorate degree from Columbia, and the last one, a photo of herself at age one wearing her cherry dress. Hetty had insisted upon hanging the framed dress next to the photo, thankfully (after a protracted argument) outside Stacey's room. She paused in front of it, contemplating another day alone. Too boring, she thought. No excitement. On a whim, she decided to find the place where they sold those famous dresses. Her mother didn't even need to know where she'd gone.

The Woman's Exchange on Clayton Road appeared, at first sight, to be an ordinary gift shop, but unlike the Ye Olde Gift Shoppe she had encountered on the way to the Ozarks, The Woman's Exchange was brimming with the finest artisanal crafts—everything from hand-painted china and smocked baby bonnets to knitted sweaters for dogs. It even had an adjacent tearoom that was filled with casually elegant women, their chatter light and demure. Stacey's eyes settled on a printed sign hanging near the cash register. *Experienced seamstresses wanted to construct garments for children. We will supply all materials.*

"I'm interested in your cherry dress," Stacey said to the

woman at the cash register. The crystal tulip brooch on the lapel of the woman's jacket resembled a family heirloom dating back to the American Revolution. Preoccupied with tallying her receipts, the woman hardly took notice of Stacey.

"Do you wish to purchase a dress or become a consignor?" She finally lifted her gaze, observing Stacey's unkempt hair, buxom hips, and rumpled sweatshirt.

"Pardon me," Stacey said. "A consign what?"

"Most of our items are sold on consignment," she said, then continued pedantically: "We don't own these items you see in the shop. We sell them for women who toiled long hours to produce them. Some of the women are refugees or battered wives, others are mothers of war amputees or the mentally unsound. 'Decayed gentlewomen' we used to call the women who sew for us."

"Sorry, I didn't know." Stacey said. "I already have a cherry dress. I just want some information on how The Woman's Exchange got started in St. Louis."

"Well, I suppose you know that we've been in business for nearly a century."

"Yes, my aunt told me."

"And the volunteers who run The Woman's Exchange are remarkable. They have had enough determination to keep this place going through the Great Depression, several recessions, and the demise of fine craftsmanship." With her authoritative pointer finger she gestured at the wealth of objects for sale in the shop.

"That's very interesting," said Stacey. "But, if you don't mind, I want to know about the seamstresses, the decayed ladies that you mentioned. Is there any way that I could meet one of them?"

"Absolutely not!" The woman seemed perturbed by the audacity of the question. "Their privacy is of the utmost importance to us."

"But… it's for my history project at school," Stacey lied.

"Good luck on your project, young lady. But you'll need to complete it without our betrayal of a long-honoured trust." And that was that. There was no point in arguing any further. Stacey could take a snooty hint. A century of unmitigated grit was not about to be upended by a teenager who hadn't done her homework and didn't appear to belong.

On the drive home, Stacey felt thwarted by what had happened at The Woman's Exchange. She wanted to tell her mother about her misadventure, like a child bringing a hurtful incident home from camp, but she doubted that her mother would be there. Flipping the radio on and off, she regretted that she hadn't bought one or two of those homemade pies— the lemon or coconut tempted her the most—to devour in her room later on. The pies were likely not kosher, but who cared? They ate shrimp in restaurants all the time and nothing terrible seemed to happen. Rush hour traffic heading west on Clayton Road was barely moving. She imagined the sugary smell of those pies, fiddled with her hair, and checked for her dad's black BMW in the rearview mirror, ever hopeful that he would come to live with them again. She fumed that The Woman's Exchange wouldn't tell her the name of just one seamstress who sewed those cherry dresses.

The sound of a sewing machine began to click in her head. She pictured a Black woman bent over her Singer, pulling white fabric under the needle. Her shoe pushed down on the foot pedal, then released it. Her calf looked like it was chained to the leg of the sewing table. Stacey imagined a boy in the room, too, the son of the seamstress. He was eating a grilled cheese sandwich while watching television. A bowl of soup sat on the TV tray in front of him. Stacey figured it was Campbell's tomato. The boy didn't speak. His mother pushed harder on the pedal, making the needle go faster and faster. She looked up at her son to reassure him of her loving presence. And in that split second, the needle pierced through her finger tip. The seamstress yanked her finger back. Blood stained the whiter-than-white cherry dress.

Stacey slammed her foot on the break, narrowly missing the bumper of the Buick in front of her. If she caused a car crash, her mother was going to be furious.

◈

May 13, 1980

Dear Diary,

I'm worried about Stacey. I keep finding Sara Lee chocolate cake boxes under her bed, and she's always going to the bathroom as soon as we've finished eating. Then I hear water gushing from the faucet, like it's Niagara Falls in there.

I'm totally anxious and can't sleep so I'm going to list here the top ten reasons why I think Lenny took off. (Better than counting sheep.)

1. Terry Sue. (My guilt, big time, over her death. Never goes away.)
2. The mystery about our survival in the Lodz ghetto. (Lenny couldn't relate. Also wasn't interested.)
3. My attachment to Mama, Papa, and my sisters despite our little disagreements. (Lenny said it was like I was living in a glue pot with them.) Of course, I'd die for my family because that's why families are supposed to do for each other. (Lenny always said, "What about me?" To be perfectly honest, I'm not sure I'd die for him.)
4. My over-protectiveness of Josh and Stacey when they were younger. (Where did all of that smothering/ mothering go? Since the divorce, I'm hardly around for Stacey anymore, like tonight. I've got to do better on that one.)
5. My irritability over small things. (Lenny was unflappable, no matter what.)

6. Difficulty sleeping (no fun). Bad sex (no fun). Clutter everywhere (no fun and a fire hazard).

7. My distrust of everyone and everything. (Especially Lenny. I never understood why he needed to buy a new BMW all of a sudden.)

Okay, I'm short a couple of reasons, but the list is long enough to sink any marriage, and I'm feeling zonked from no sleep. So if I'm such a genius with the reasons, why didn't I do something sooner to fix the problems? That's the $64,000 question, alright, and I can't answer it myself.

Always,
Hetty

Toni

Toni STOOD IN THE MINISCULE entranceway to her fifth-floor walk-up. She had rushed back from St. Louis in order to be in New York when her two guests from Japan were scheduled to arrive. They—Kenji Sato and Kazuo Kobayashi—knew Toni's friend, Cameron Landry, who had once taught English in Osaka. Kenji and Kazuo had been his students. The three had stayed in touch.

"They're jolly good guys," Cam had told her. "And their English is quite good. You'll get along famously."

"Don't try to butter me up," Toni had said. "I don't mind showing them around while you're at the political science conference." Now she watched the two Japanese guests bow slightly in front of her, palms of their hands flat against their thighs, hips hinging, feet pressed together with the toes of their sneakers perfectly aligned.

"It's a small world," Toni said to them.

"Small world?" Kenji replied, knitting his sparse eyebrows together. He had a wiry body, chiseled features, and strong hands. The artistic one, she thought.

"You must be Kenji," she said.

He nodded. Both guests began to slip off their shoes.

"Never mind," Toni said. "That's not necessary." She glanced at the auburn streaks in the more cherubic guy's hair. "And that makes you Kazuo." The creases at the corners of his eyes were the only sign of his age. She smiled. With their crisp jeans and limited-edition sneakers, these two Japanese guys, barely pushing forty, projected a cool cosmopolitanism that intrigued her.

Before long, they were perched on stools around Toni's makeshift kitchen table—later that evening it would revert to a bathtub—drinking the matcha green tea that they had brought her. Toni laid out dried figs, apricots and a bowl of sunflower seeds. She wasn't used to being a host, but she had managed to coax a few tips from Hetty before leaving St. Louis. She twirled their gift of chopsticks between her fingers, doubting that she would ever be able to use them in the proper way. She'd rather starve than eat a grain of rice like a clumsy oaf, especially under their scrutiny. Kazuo tactfully took the chopsticks from her and began lifting the sunflower seeds one by one from her glazed bowl to his lips, as if extracting smooth pebbles from a stony beach. The nutty smell of roasted rice rose from their tea cups.

Then Kazuo pulled a final gift from the yellow bag he had left at his feet, presenting it to Toni with both hands. Toni felt pink splotches developing on her face as she accepted the box, more conscious than usual that gift-giving rituals had never taken hold in the Berk family. She couldn't recall any birthday presents that she had received throughout her childhood, not even the last one from Mama before she died.

"Very small gift," Kazuo said to ease her obvious embarrassment. She manoeuvred the object out of its cubic container. Okay, she thought, I'm supposed to know what this is. But her brain felt as thick as fudge. She stared at the bell suspended in what looked like a bamboo bird cage. The spindles of the cage were so close together that she could hardly squeeze her thumbnail between them. From the bell hung a long oblong streamer, dyed in shades of blue, ranging from a bright azure to a deep indigo.

"The wind makes the bell chime like this." Kazuo flicked the cage with a boyish ping to make a tinkling sound. Toni noticed a glint of delight in his smile. She squinted at the tiny white cats printed on his navy button-down shirt, hundreds of them curled up with their eyes shut. "Are your cats sleeping?" she asked.

"No, they are thinking." He spoke in a sheepish tone, lacing his fingers together and stretching out his arms. "About how to find my future wife."

"Let's not talk about your ghost wife," Kenji said, blushing on Kazuo's behalf. Kenji, more gregarious and confident, seemed to have little difficulty finding partners. Without prompting, he divulged that he'd been engaged twice.

Galaxy at that moment sprung from the top of the fridge onto the bathtub tabletop. The cat's tail swished forcefully across the bowl of sunflower seeds and scattered the tiny morsels onto the kitchen floor.

Toni did not believe in ghosts or phantoms or any of that hocus pocus stuff. She had little interest in Kazuo's prized possession, a vintage red Mercedes-Benz which he referred to as his sweetie pie. The very term 'sweetie pie' made her cringe. She had never heard of Hayao Miyazaki, the Japanese master of animation, whom Kenji and Kazuo idolized. Her taste in cinema favoured the French New Wave directors, such as Jean-Luc Godard and Francois Truffaut. She had seen Truffaut's *Jules et Jim* three times, hypnotized each time by Jeanne Moreau singing "Le Tourbillon." (After the third viewing, Toni began to wear her hair in a French roll, just like Moreau's, and bought a black-and-white striped sweater similar to Moreau's in the film.) Yet, despite their differences— she suspected it was because of their differences—Kenji and Kazuo appealed to her. They were smart, attractive, funny, and, she calculated, available in their own way. Almost immediately, she decided that one of them would be the father of her child.

About an hour later, Kazuo excused himself to go to the

bathroom. On his return, he announced, "Your bathroom door doesn't close properly. I'll fix it for you." He rubbed his bare foot back and forth on the Persian area rug covering a patch of the concrete floor.

"Now?" Toni had never noticed the gap between the bathroom door and the frame. Living in a tenement that was about a century old, she was relieved to have a private, indoor toilet and a bathroom sink. "Can it wait another hundred years? I won't sneak a peek while you're in there," she said. "Promise."

"Where's your tool kit?"

"Tool kit?" She had never lived in a house with tools. Papa and Mama didn't own a hammer or nails. She herself wouldn't know what to do with them.

"All I need is a screwdriver," Kazuo said. He cocked his head to the side and smiled.

"Uh, sorry." She stared at her feet, hoping he wouldn't notice her embarrassment.

"Okay," Kenji interjected. He extended his legs, as if he felt restless. "Time for a walk." Before they could disagree, he began to hustle them out the front door, racing them down the stairs. At the corner of East 27th and Lexington, he announced that he had a new girlfriend whom he had promised to meet at midnight. Toni and Kazuo watched him sail down the semi-deserted street.

"Now I get it." Toni laughed as she and Kazuo walked past the closed European bakery and D'Agostino's, floating toward each other, then drifting away.

"I like your oval face," Kazuo whispered into her hair, "but I'm not sure I am capable of loving anybody."

His directness surprised her. "Are you sure you're Japanese?"

"Very Japanese." He lifted her free hand to his mouth and kissed her wrist, licking the salt off her sweaty skin.

She started to hum the song from *Jules and Jim* as they walked up the steps to her apartment, Toni leading the way.

Her hand reached backwards as if to tug Kazuo up the dimly lit stairwell. On the third-floor landing, she smelled something frying, like liver and onions. It could be her neighbour having a late, late dinner or an early, early breakfast, she thought. That's what she loved about Manhattan.

Around two a.m., only a few hours after they first met, Toni and Kazuo sponged each other in her bathtub. The warm water trickled between her breasts. He followed the drip with his finger. Later, he told her that his name meant harmonious in Japanese. She wasn't surprised. He entered her so gently that she gave in with none of her usual resistance. She inhaled deeply, his scent mingling with the clean smell of Ivory soap. He held her, making low, soothing sounds while she quietly cried, "Baby."

◈

May 14, 1980

I just heard from Linda Sue who phoned to tell me that Marion called Papa's house. She was apparently looking for me, and when Linda Sue said I wasn't there, she started asking questions about my whereabouts. Ha! Linda Sue would be the last person on earth I'd confide in. I should tell my innocent kid sister that I left Papa, Hetty and her in St. Louis to entertain some Japanese guys that I didn't even know. Oh, please. What kind of sister does Marion think I am? Which raises the whole question of what a good sister really is. Not sure I have an answer for that at the moment, but I do know what sisterhood is all about. It means women sharing a common goal and working collectively to make the world a better place. Unfortunately, sisters by blood and sisters by choice don't always align.

In solidarity,
Toni

◈

"*Moshi moshi.*" The words were slurred together, delivered quickly and melodiously, like a song.

"Hello," Toni said. "Who's calling?" It was only two days since she'd met the Japanese guys, and their voices were indistinguishable.

"It's Kenji. Remember me?"

"Very well. How are you enjoying New York?"

"It's good," he said.

"Great."

"Uh..." He took a long drag on his cigarette and exhaled. "Mind if I come to see you today? Some of my art is in Japanese museums. I will bring my portfolio."

"Sorry, I'm busy."

"All day?"

"Most of the day. I'm teaching."

"No breaks?" He coughed.

"Yes, I do have an afternoon break."

"I'll come then. Is it okay?"

"Umm... sure, okay."

As soon as she finished her early afternoon lecture, Toni hurried up Lex and bought a few Danishes at the European bakery to serve with tea, relieved that she had cleaned Galaxy's litter box before departing for the university that morning.

◈

May 16, 1980

Kenji is an amazing artist. I was totally blown away by the photos of his sculpture, though I can't say the sex was anything to write home about. Sometimes things just happen (if you let them). I barely managed to get back to my office, pick up a bunch of exams to return to my students, grab my lecture notes, and arrive, breathless, in time for my 5 o'clock class. Whew!

Yours in sisterhood,
Toni

Linda Sue

L INDA SUE STOOD AT HER DESK at the end of the school
week without so much as a rasp in her voice or a hint of
a migraine. She offered a silent prayer to the acoustic ceiling
and oversized windows in her classroom that helped her to
remain sane and healthy. The daily sound of shuffling feet and
rustling homework was mostly absorbed. Natural daylight
regularly blessed her fifth graders' dazzling faces.

Watching them file out of Room 210, Linda Sue felt content
in this imposing brick edifice, a throwback to an earlier era in
architectural design. Romanesque Revival, she thought it was
called. But it didn't matter. For her, Thornview was simply a
special place. She gathered her marking for the weekend and
walked down the empty hallway toward the steps. Already
her students' precious problems were beginning to fade
away. Until Monday morning, she would not have to think
about Kevin Brody's lost notebook or his anger management
issues or the Tootsie Rolls he devoured at lunch that made
him hyperactive for the rest of the day. (He was apparently
an angel at home. She'd been told that he loved to vacuum
the rugs and make double-decker bologna sandwiches with
pickles and chips.) How often she had descended these steps,
clutching the smooth railing with her free hand! She imagined
herself at a Meet the Teacher Night eight or ten years from
now saying to a keen parent, I still remember teaching your

older daughter, Samantha. She sat right over there. Delightful student, she was. Where is she now? And in thirty-something years, Linda Sue saw herself closing the door to Room 210 forever, still able to remember her first day in that same classroom as a fifth grader herself.

◈

June 13, 1980

Dear me,

Finally heard from Peter. He sent me this poem by Julian Tuwim, a Jewish poet born in Lodz. I guess Peter wanted to draw my attention to the Polish/Jewish connection. I get it. He said every Polish child knows this poem by heart. His mother always read it when she put him to bed, then kissed him on the nose and turned off the light. I wonder if our kids would love the poem, too. I could read it to them in English, then Peter could read it to them in Polish. He'd be a good father, I bet. I'm stapling my favourite part of the poem to this page so I don't lose it or forget him, as if I ever will.

Toodle-oo for now,
LS.

The Locomotive

A big locomotive has pulled into town,
Heavy, humongous, with sweat rolling down,
A plump jumbo olive.
Huffing and puffing and panting and smelly,
Fire belches forth from her fat cast-iron belly.

Poof, how she's burning,
Oof, how she's boiling,
Puff, how she's churning,
Huff, how she's toiling.
She's fully exhausted and all out of breath,
Yet the coalman continues to stoke her to death.

Hetty

HETTY LINGERED OVER her oatmeal, sipping orange juice between mouthfuls, checking the date on the wall calendar, delaying as long as possible her departure for Papa's. She detested the clunk of her glass on the table. The sound of glass on glass shattered her nerves in the morning. Come to think of it, she also detested the round shape of the table. A rectangular table would suit this breakfast nook far better, she mused, regretting, as always, that she hadn't become an interior decorator. She was a firm believer in the transformative power of well-designed living spaces. By the simple act of moving a sofa from one corner of the room to another, she was convinced that a person could alter her life. The round table, the more she studied it, looked like out-of-place patio furniture in her kitchen, lacking only an umbrella and a hole in the middle. Her mind was made up. She must switch back to wood. And change the wrought-iron chairs, too. New cushions. A different colour scheme. The whole shebang. She'd go shopping on the way home from U. City.

When Hetty had first moved to Frontenac, she checked on Papa every other day, but she no longer felt compelled to drive back and forth so frequently. Now twice a week seemed sufficient—in fact, more than enough with one of those days being Friday for Shabbat dinner. The trouble was that U. City depressed her. The Loop, once a lively enclave of Orthodox Jewish families like the Berks, had changed. She would be lucky to find a kosher butcher there now. Not that Hetty, strictly speaking, required a kosher butcher. But, for the sake of tradition, she would like to know that Mr. Frankel was still there instead of the health food store, the bike shop, the co-op grocery, the print gallery, and the hole in the wall selling old movie posters. A person could forget about trying to find a jar of baby food in the open-air market, not that Hetty needed a jar of baby food. The Loop catered to students from Wash U. now and the few older people still living there. She emptied her oatmeal down the garbage disposal, put her bowl in the dishwasher, and, glancing at the forsythia hedge at the back of her garden, wondered why she had so few flowers when her neighbour just a short distance away had beautiful yellow blooms. She dialled Papa's phone number to tell him she was on her way.

Hetty's nerves, already jittery when she turned right onto Tulane, became more frayed at the sight of the *For Sale* sign on the Krammers' front lawn, two doors east of Papa's house. As soon as she parked the car, she grabbed the sugarless gum in her glove compartment and popped two pieces into her mouth, which felt as dry as sawdust. No issue in U. City was considered more controversial, confusing, and divisive than real estate. The sale of any home could tip the racial balance of the community and result in plummeting property values, or so it was whispered across backyard fences and in the aisles of the local Schnucks supermarket. Hetty tried to remain calm, but she found herself shaking as she jammed the key into the deadbolt on Papa's front door.

◈

July 14, 1980

Dear Diary,

Papa has got to sell. Period. Before it's too late. I won't be as sneaky as that agent from Centurion 84, hiring a Black woman to push a baby carriage along Midland Boulevard. What a gross trick to scare people into thinking that the area is becoming one big black ghetto and they better sell fast to get their money out. I'm a little more ethical than that. But he is my father, and he's not safe where he is. Of course, Tilya and Linda Sue would totally disagree because they don't give a fig about what is happening in the housing market. It's sometimes hard to believe that we are sisters.

Always,
Hetty

Toni

TONI FELT THE WARMTH of the morning light streaming into the Nissan, filtered by the smoke from Kazuo's second cigarette of the ride. Those auburn streaks in his hair, so seductive in New York, were quickly fading in Osaka under an acrid haze of tobacco. Outside, bikes whizzed past, their smooth glide punctured by small yellow dots that bobbed up and down. As they got closer, Toni noticed that these little specks of brightness were children wearing wide brimmed hats, being pedalled to school by their parents. A throng of other cyclists—a uniformed schoolboy, a man ferrying groceries, a woman transporting a very happy little dog—were riding on the sidewalks that they shared with pedestrians. Above, but in clear view, futons hung from laundry poles on sunny apartment balconies, and freshly washed clothes flapped in the summer air.

Kenji slammed his foot on the brake to avoid the car zigzagging in front of them. They were taking her to a hotel for breakfast. Toni listened to the guys speaking Japanese, but she didn't have the foggiest notion of what they were saying to each other. Her backpack rested on the seat next to her, bulging with a used Japanese phrasebook, which she hadn't bothered to open, and a travel guide on short-term loan from Cameron Landry. Kazuo twisted around to translate for her, his eyes shaded by sunglasses. The dark lenses made him (and everyone else on earth) instantly more attractive.

"So, have you found your future wife yet?" she asked him as Kenji pulled the Nissan into the hotel garage.

"He has lots of future wives," Kenji answered as they walked toward the hotel. "They are scattered all over the map." He held the heavy glass door of the hotel open for her, always polite in a self-mocking sort of way.

"Melbourne?" Toni asked Kazuo speculatively.

"Melbourne," he confirmed, then added, "Brisbane."

"Sydney?" Toni queried. "Madrid?"

"Barcelona," Kazuo said, gaining momentum. "Seville, Granada, Bilbao."

"Paris?" After a while, the cities began to sound like the names of real women, Kazuo's international band of lovers— Paris Chevalier, Sydney Smith—who wrenched him out of his everyday loneliness. At that point, the little game Toni and Kazuo were playing ceased to be a fun thing to do. When they arrived, she felt his hand on the back of her upper arm, steering her through the hotel lobby. His eyes were still hidden by sunglasses, which provided a scaffolding for his soft-featured, sad face.

◈

The guys wanted Toni to experience a traditional Japanese breakfast while she was visiting them in Osaka, the kind of lavish spreads offered at upscale hotels in Japan. Toni was staying in the spare room of Kenji's colleague, Fumiko, whose life was a torrent of art installations, interviews, and travel with no time to put more than milk, cereal, and moldy strawberries on the table each morning, kindly. Her silky black hair bounced down her back; her chest was so thin it was practically translucent. Toni felt elephantine in her presence.

"Stunning," Toni said at the sight of the hotel buffet. The artful interplay of colour, shadow, white space, and lacquered boxes aroused all of her senses. She couldn't identify most of the food spread out before them, but she wanted all of it in her mouth if not in her stomach.

"Everything is very light," Kazuo said. "The food doesn't weigh heavy here." He jiggled his belly with his hands. "Start with soup. It lubricates the throat and stimulates the appetite."

"No, try the eel," Kenji said.

"Maybe later...." Toni stared at the turnips and seaweed. She returned to their table by herself with a cup of green tea to soothe her rumbling gut. So she couldn't understand Japanese and would never indulge in eel for breakfast. Who cared? But that wasn't the point. She felt like a foreigner, a distinct outsider in Japan, a feeling that threatened her to the core, her Tilya Berkowitz core, the core she had tried to leave in Lodz but couldn't, the core that understood an ever-present fact: what happened to Jews before could happen again. She looked at her watch, trying to calculate local St. Louis time, feeling caught in the grey space between here and there. She continued to ruminate. What was Papa doing while she braced herself for a breakfast of fermented soybeans with two Japanese guys in Osaka?

"Are you sure you can't come to Hiroshima with me?" she asked from the backseat of the Nissan. They were on their way to drop her off at Shin-Osaka station. She had planned to travel to Hiroshima alone, but after breakfast she felt rootless and in need of companionship.

"Sorry, can't today," Kazuo said. "Maybe we could see the Hanshin Tigers play at Koshien Stadium some other time. Everyone Japanese loves baseball, you know. And the dirt at Koshien... it's sacred."

"Really?" she asked, recalling the only time she had attended a Cardinals game at Busch Stadium in St. Louis. Lenny had orchestrated that family outing before his marriage to Hetty, back when Terry Sue was still alive and Mama was still able to leave the house like a sane person. Lenny chose to ignore the fact that none of the Berks liked baseball or knew the rules of the game. Like a true *mensch* and dentist, he struggled to explain the infield fly rule to Papa, who was just getting the hang of pop flies and couldn't grasp the intricacies of forced outs, double and triple plays, or foul lines. "*Narishkeit,*" Papa had said. "Since when can infidels fly?"

Mama, Toni recalled, had spent the game worrying about one of her daughters choking on the dreck that was sold for snacks at the ballpark. When Terry Sue tossed a crackerjack into her mouth and then began to cough, Mama whipped her finger down Terry Sue's throat, forcing her to regurgitate the caramel-coated popcorn into the palm of her mother's tremulous hand.

"Koshien. It is very sacred," Kenji said. "Your Babe Ruth once played there."

"Interesting." If Toni was supposed to feel some sort of attachment to Babe Ruth, she hated to disappoint them. She didn't even know the name of the team Babe Ruth had played for or the position. That's how American she wasn't.

"Sorry, I don't want to visit Hiroshima," Kenji said. She looked for his eyes in the rearview mirror, but his attention was fixed on the road. He was scanning the frantic movement of trucks, cars, and motorcycles vying for space on room. "When I was in school, the past stopped at about 1925. The teacher told us to read the rest of the textbook on our own over the summer."

"Yeah," Kazuo said, taking a cigarette out of the pack in his shirt pocket. "It was almost a forbidden topic in my school. And my parents never talked about it."

"Very complicated." Kenji nodded his head as if to end the conversation.

"I could never skip over World War II like that," Toni said. She stared out the window at the flock of people crossing the street. Osaka, Kazuo had told her, was once the commercial capital of Japan. No kidding. She had never seen so many department stores, covered shopping arcades, stalls, and boutiques jammed together. She turned her gaze to the sweat glistening on the back of their necks. "Where I come from, memory defines us. It's who we are, you know. It's what holds us together."

"Sometimes to forget is not really to forget," Kazuo said as their car stopped at the curb in front of the station. He jumped out of the front seat and sprung the rear door of the Nissan open for her. "You are on platform six. Hurry." He slung her backpack over his shoulder, grabbed her hand, and ran with her into the station.

The wide, well-lit aisles of Shin-Osaka station were crammed with stalls selling an array of pre-packaged lunchboxes, tastefully wrapped sweets, and souvenirs of all kinds. Toni took a fast glance at the keyrings, fans, chopsticks, and origami paper. Osaka is a shopping addict's paradise, she noted, sure that Hetty would be in heaven here, but surprised that her sister had suddenly popped into her mind. *Who invited Hetty to come along?*

"Hurry," Kazuo said again. "Trains in Japan run exactly on time." Harried salary men wearing black suits, blindingly white shirts, and gleaming dress shoes hurtled toward the train platforms, undeterred by the heat. Kazuo rustled his shirt to fan off the sweat dripping from his chest. Just before she stepped onto the train, he wrapped his arms around her and pulled her snugly into him. She couldn't breathe. A moan of pleasure seeped out of him, tinged with a whimper of despair.

⁂

Hiroshima was not at all what Toni expected. On this summer day, it looked strikingly like a tourist spot with wide paved boulevards and sun-dappled buildings, one of those new towns where nothing was more than a couple of decades old, a city delicately balanced between absence and presence. As soon as she found a seat on the tram going to the Hiroshima Peace Memorial Park, she opened her backpack and removed

Cameron's water-stained Japan travel guide. "Don't drop it in any more puddles," he had said just before leaving her at JFK airport. "And if you lose it, don't replace it with a Fodor's. Absolutely no dice." Toni gave the travel guidebook a little pat as if to reassure Cam on the other side of the ocean that his prized possession was safe and dry.

Resting her backpack on the tram floor, Toni fumbled through the travel guide, glancing at some photos. She flipped to a page that Cam had folded back in the upper corner and read the solemn words:

The name Hiroshima will signify for all time the catastrophic tragedy of war and the horrific potential for nuclear annihilation that has loomed in human affairs since the fatal day in August, 1945, when an atomic weapon was first used over that southwestern Japanese city.

Outside the tram window, a green ribbon of grass flowed alongside the bustling avenues of rebuilt Hiroshima. Toni reread the words in the guidebook. Until this minute, Hiroshima hadn't signified much to her. She knew next to nothing about the Pacific War or the wartime atrocities committed by the United States in East Asia. In her education, the subject of Hiroshima had been treated as a memory sinkhole. She struggled to recall a single time that any aspect of the Pacific War was even mentioned in her modern history class at U. City High. And in university, wartime atrocities tended to be discussed from a European perspective.

Toni forced herself to look at the older Japanese faces on the tram, then quickly turned away and shifted her gaze downward to Cam's travel guide, continuing to read: *The Americans dropped the atomic bomb on Hiroshima in 1945 to bring a speedy end to the war and save lives.*

In the margin, Cam had written "very doubtful," and further down, he had scribbled "whose lives were saved?" He had also inserted an article from an academic journal right between the pages of the guidebook. An eye-witness account quoted in the article caught Toni's attention:

Yumi: There was no one who looked like a human being. There were no normal faces. The skin of my hands was peeled and hanging down. There were people whose entrails were hanging from their bodies, people without legs, and people who couldn't utter a sound, their bodies and clothes burning. Some people tried to put their entrails back into their bodies. That's why even now I can't eat a sausage.

Toni couldn't bear to look again at the older riders on the tram. She didn't want to confront the thick scars she had seen on one woman's hands and face. She felt a stab of guilt as she stretched her unblemished hands over the page to hide the words, then tapped her fingers up and down, as if she were playing a Chopin polonaise. She was always told she had the slender, lovely fingers of a pianist. A cursory glance at her hands—that was all it took to remind her of the obvious: she had survived with no outward scars. The Japanese survivors of Hiroshima were not so lucky. Their trauma was visible in old wounds that could still be seen, suffering made public and calcified into a lasting identity. Toni closed the travel guide and stuffed it into her backpack. When the tram arrived at the Peace Memorial Park, she exited with the other chatty tourists from Australia, England, and, as it happened, Brooklyn. For once, their familiar Brooklynese sounded comforting.

Surprisingly, there were no ashes in an urn marking the spot where the bomb had exploded. Only a small stone plaque was installed on the ground directly underneath the point of detonation to commemorate the blast. Not far from the plaque stood the half-exploded brick building with its canonical metal dome intact. All other evidence of the A-bomb's devastation was invisible to the eye. Only the brain engaged in the reconstructive work of memory. Toni stood there surrounded by hills on nearly every side which shaped the city into a deep bowl. What a majestic place Hiroshima was on a peaceful summer day. Closing her eyes in the stillness, she imagined an exploding flash and boom over the middle of the bowl, torching every inch of the low flat delta with fire. When she listened hard, she could hear the countless cries for help welling up from the earth beneath her.

Toni bent down to touch the ground, pinching a bit of loose soil between her unblemished fingers, curious, as the dirt slid into her palm, about the families of Kenji and Kazuo. She walked the short distance to the museum, sickened, as she toured the exhibit, by the burnt personal effects of the victims: watches, clothing, hair. Where had Kenji and Kazuo's parents and grandparents been at 8:15 on that morning in August? It would be rude to ask them. It was too late to apologize for what had happened, but she said sorry anyway.

⁕

August 12, 1980

I am totally exhausted from the trip to Hiroshima. So shut down, I can barely think. And—wouldn't you know it?—Fumiko was home when I got back. What timing! We hadn't managed to spend more than twenty minutes together during my entire visit, but now, when I could hardly keep my head up from fatigue, she offered to make tea for us. *Oy!* I felt I had to accept. And while the tea was steeping and my head was swimming in guilt and shame and confusion, she asked me if I was a feminist. The absolute furthest topic from my mind at that moment. Kenji and Kazuo must have told her that I was into women's rights, which Cam must have told them. I had certainly said nothing to Kenji and Kazuo about women or rights, and they would never have guessed that I had an ounce of feminism in me from my behaviour since I met them. That's for sure. Most of my previous conversations with Fumiko focused on her paintings, so I was a bit taken aback—and exhausted.

Actually, I have been thinking about women's issues in

107

Japan. The other day I had some spare time on the train back from Tokyo and tried to write a letter to Marion about the status of women here. I realized very quickly that I don't have much to say. I haven't contacted the women's lib activists that I thought I would (and still should). The truth is I'm finding it impossible to follow Japanese news and current events. News? What news? In the end, I tore up the letter to Marion and sent her a postcard of Atsuko Tanaka's Electric Dress that I bought at the museum shop in Tokyo. I omitted the fact that Tanaka risked electrocution when she first exhibited—I mean "performed"—the dress made of hundreds of flashing lightbulbs connected by a great mass of wires. On the back of the postcard to Marion, I wrote the motto of the artists' collective Tanaka belonged to: *Do something that no one before you has done.* Because I know that Marion can relate to that. Fumiko and I didn't talk much about feminism over our tea. I was too exhausted to string three sentences together, and there's the language gap anyway. But I did say to her (and maybe I shouldn't have been so honest) that I found it odd that Japan is one of the most industrialized countries in the world, yet the sexes seem to be unequal.

Fumiko did not seem so happy about this, though her smile never wavered.

Home soon,
Yours in sisterhood,
Toni

⬖

"What's this?" Toni asked Kazuo when he handed her a sheet of paper, an elongated rectangle embossed with an intricate gold leaf pattern. They were sitting in Osaka Castle Park, not far from his apartment, their last time together before she was scheduled to fly back to New York.

"It's a poem slip. In old Japan, poem slips were hung on the branches of flowering cherry trees to celebrate spring."

"Nice," she said. "I'm not aware of that custom in the West."

"Read the poem," he said. She heard an impish mirth in his voice, unexpected and the opposite of her sober feelings of resignation.

"Did you write it?" She asked.

"No, it's a waka, an ancient Japanese form of poetry. Just five lines."

She read the last three phrases aloud. "Some memories/ like putting on/ dirty socks."

They fell silent. Around them people were enjoying picnics and young boys were tossing a ball around on the baseball diamond.

Toni burst out laughing and tipped her head onto his shoulder.

"Why are you laughing?" he asked, kissing her hair.

"Because that waka writer nailed it."

◈

August 18, 1980

What the hell?! Extending my stay in Japan until classes begin in September. Can't tear myself away from Kazuo now.

Yours in sisterhood,
Toni

Hetty

THE LAST TIME HETTY SET EYES on Josh must have been a year ago. Possibly even longer. After university he drifted out to California, like many of his high school friends who either went east or west. The muddy middle—St. Louis, to be more precise—had a lot less to offer. Sure, Hetty planned to speak with Josh every Sunday morning, but as months of separation turned into years, their long-distance calls became harder to maintain. To be honest, the time difference between San Francisco and Frontenac baffled her. It was the same problem with Toni in New York. Was New York one hour ahead or behind St. Louis time? Then there was Osaka. Hetty didn't even try to calculate the time difference between here and there. Waiting for Linda Sue to arrive with Chinese take-out for dinner on a muggy night in August, Hetty toyed with the idea of installing various clocks in her bedroom, configuring different time zones around the world. Best to avoid Roman numerals, she conceded, but it struck her that a jacquard bedspread and matching drapes would go well with three or four antique clocks. She wondered why all of the Berks couldn't be on local time. She meant, of course, her time.

Linda Sue didn't tell Hetty about the letter she had recently received from Josh until they had finished with their fortune cookies. Hetty read what was written on her slip of paper first. "Land is always on the mind of a flying bird." She broke off half of the crispy cookie and stuck it into her mouth. "What's that supposed to mean?"

"It means you are only as good as your last sale." Linda Sue got up from the table and went to the counter where she'd left her purse next to slimy packets of dribbling soy and plum sauce.

"You are such a damn no-*goodnik* sometimes," Hetty said, rereading her paper fortune. "That's not at all what it means. You think you're so superior just because you don't have to sell anything to put bread on the table."

Linda Sue unzipped the outer compartment of her purse, fished out an envelope, and pretended to fan herself with it. "It's a letter from Josh. Want to hear it?"

Hetty drew a hurried breath that betrayed her indignation. She was wearing makeup that looked a shade too dark for her and dragged down the features on her face. The concealer, thickly applied, resembled mocha almond fudge ice cream pressed into a lumpy bagel. "He writes to you and not to me," she complained.

"Okay. Forget about it," Linda Sue said and began to read the letter out loud.

Dearest Aunt Linda,

I hope you are not too mad at me for not writing sooner. I've been incredibly busy mounting an exhibit of my Lodz ghetto photos. I have to admit that ever since our trip to Poland, the only thing I really have wanted to do with my life is to be a photographer, like Mendel Grossman. I want to leave some sort of a record, like he did, before the memories of the Jews of Poland fade into history. Maybe I suffer from not having suffered enough. True or false? You are the teacher, Auntie Linda.

Now whatever you think about me, please don't have a complete fit when I tell you what I did. Last year right after the High Holy Days, I started asking my friends for the names of their tattoo artists in San Francisco. Of course, everyone I asked swore that his tattoo artist was the most detailed, the cleanest, and the best respected tattoo artist in the business. On the first Saturday after the Day of Atonement, I went to a place called Mermaids on Mission Street and had a big yellow butterfly tattooed across my left shoulder. Here's a photo that I took of it. Very cool, if I do say so myself.

Fly free.

Your adorable nephew,
Josh

Linda Sue folded the letter, put it back in her purse and gave the photo of Josh with his yellow butterfly tattoo to Hetty. "I'm sure you'll want to frame this," she said, checking her watch, then kissing her sister on both cheeks before she departed for home.

◈

August 20, 1980

Dear Diary,

I love Linda Sue, but did she really need to share that letter from Josh with me? Not that I believe for one minute that she read me the whole letter. I saw her eyes skimming the page. You know, sometimes the people in my family just don't understand. For instance, my two sisters who don't have children of their own. They don't understand the disappointment parents feel about some of the choices their kids make. A son with a tattoo of a butterfly. Don't ask. When he comes to St. Louis next, he can wear a button-down shirt that will cover the whole thing. And I'm hiding the photo under my mattress. Frame it! Is she nuts? Nobody else has a kid with a tattoo.

Oy vey iz mir.

Always,
Hetty

Toni

THE TING STARTLED HER. Toni's hand collided with the Japanese wind chime hanging in her window as she tried to let in some fresh air. No more denial. She was back. Back on East 27th Street. Back on the fifth floor of her walk-up. Back in New York where people routinely shoved food into their mouths in public spaces—the smellier and runnier, the better. Hot dogs, pretzels, and knishes didn't even raise an eyebrow. She sighed. How different from Japan where people rarely ate while walking outside. She should have known that coming back would not be easy. If a little pill existed to cure the awful feeling of culture shock in reverse, she would have swallowed it without hesitation.

Galaxy jumped onto the desk under the window and rubbed against Toni's bare arm tentatively, as if to say *welcome home* and *why in the hell did you leave me in the first place?* "Silly Mr. Kid Cat," she said to Galaxy. "I know Cam took good care of you." That morning, when he'd returned Galaxy, howling blue murder, Toni didn't have a chance to talk with him. Cam was rushing up to the Bronx to console his mother whose diabetes was causing her leg pain. She hadn't returned his trusty travel guidebook yet nor given him the tin of green tea she bought for him at Shin-Osaka station. She ached for Kazuo and Kenji, particularly in the kitchen. It was like visiting a Buddhist temple in Japan where the history of the place and the presence of people who walked there centuries ago could still be felt. She opened the fridge and unscrewed the lid on a lone jar of tomato sauce to discover a froth of moldy bubbles floating in the thickened red liquid. How long would this grungy kitchen with a claw-foot bathtub strike her as a Buddhist temple? Fully dressed, her suitcase still unpacked, she flopped down on her bed, uncomfortably aware of the constricting waistband on her khaki pants and the beginning of the semester the next day.

Late in the night, the phone rang. She fumbled for the receiver, knocking it out of its cradle and onto the floor. "Tilya, are you there? Tilya!"

"I'm here. I just got back," Toni said, sounding irritable as she usually did with her sisters. "Anything important or can I call you tomorrow?" She glanced at her clock radio sitting on a milk crate across the room. It was 1:04 in the morning—an hour earlier in St. Louis, a day later in Japan.

"Sure, it can wait until tomorrow because there's nothing you can do about it now."

Tilya detected a smug tone in her older sibling's voice. "Nothing I can do about what?"

"Papa died last week," Hetty said. "When you were in Japan."

She felt her heart hammering and small bumps forming on her arms. "And you didn't call me? I left you Fumiko's number."

"Sorry, Tilya. A heart attack. You were a million miles from here. There was no way you could have gotten back in time. We weren't even sure of your new arrival date." That line of defence would continue to be offered for years to come, as well as other variations on the theme of Tilya's bad timing, her preference for being as far away as possible from them, and the guilt she should feel during every waking moment of every day of her life for deserting her family.

"What about a telegram?"

"We didn't want to disturb you...." Hetty was silent for a

few moments. "We did everything according to Jewish law, as Papa would have wanted. It's forbidden to put off the burial and shiva unnecessarily, you know."

"So his second daughter's presence was somehow deemed unnecessary." Tilya winced and searched the bedroom for Galaxy. "Is that what you are telling me?"

"You know," Hetty said in a huff, "everything is not always about you."

Tilya became quiet. "Just tell me, did Josh get there in time?"

"Of course he did," Hetty said as if that was the most ridiculous question imaginable. "He gave the eulogy based on the artist's statement he wrote for one of his photography shows. You know, his exhibit of the tombstones from the Jewish cemetery in Lodz I told you about?" Tilya snapped her top and bottom teeth together and started grinding them. As a final dig, Hetty added, "Maybe you don't remember because you weren't paying much attention."

"Tell Josh to send me the eulogy," Tilya said. "I'll call Linda Sue myself."

Dial tone.

⁂

September 7, 1980

Papa, will you ever forgive me for not being there for you? I would have walked on water to get back to St. Louis, if only I had known that you had suffered a sudden heart attack. Really and truly, I would have come back. I would have found a way to make it back in time. You saved us. And Hetty and I don't even know half the story. Of course I would have come home. For all these years, what happened in Poland was locked away in your memory, recorded by no one, stored in no archive. Don't think I didn't see how you felt. After every knock on the door on Tulane, I saw you peer out, as if you were expecting to be arrested—or to have one of us taken away. You, a small man with a gaunt face who always seemed to me supernaturally gentle and old. Well, your memories are history now, those encumbrances which were uniquely yours, the deepest truth about who we are: all of it is buried with you.

My worst regret—and I have a lot of them—is that I didn't get to tell you that I am going to have a baby. Already the zipper on my favourite corduroy pants stalls at the little bulge in my stomach. I wish you were here to let out the seams because I absolutely refuse to wear those ugly maternity pants with stretchy belly panels. I have the urge to tear off my corduroy pants and shred them with my bare hands. If only ripping pants or hair or flesh would make me feel less angry or miss you any less.

Anyway, I'm attaching part of Josh's eulogy to this page of my diary. It's about what he discovered on his trip to Poland, that time he first went with Linda Sue. What a *mensch* Josh has become.

Goodbye, Papa. I'll never forget you.

Tilya

Cemeteries are meant to be final resting places for our loved ones. Sometimes, though, the dead come back. At the Jewish cemetery in Lodz, standing among the tombstones, crooked and toppled over, faded and chipped, covered in moss and mould, I felt the hold of my ancestors. In the Ghetto Field, where thousands of Jewish victims were buried without headstones, I felt their hands reach out to grip mine. And at the trench along the outer wall of the cemetery, inside the gate, I heard the shovels of a small band of remaining Jews from the Lodz ghetto ordered by the Nazis to dig their own mass grave. If the Russian army had not advanced, they would have perished, every last man. I imagine that one of those starving, nearly dead trench diggers was my zaidie, Szymon Berkowicz.

Linda Sue

LINDA SUE SWEPT THE KITCHEN floor, furiously forcing the nylon bristles of her broom under the stove to catch crumbs from her quiche crust that had landed there yesterday. Since Papa's death months ago, she had succumbed to a cleaning frenzy. She had purchased the original Windex glass cleaner and the special Windex glass cleaner designed for outdoor use to ensure that the windows of her house sparkled. Her elbows ached from swiping paper towels back and forth. By the time she completed the chore, the thirty-day mourning period was behind her. Not a streak could be seen on a single windowpane. But all the scrubbing, wiping, and buffing, she admitted after weeks of cleaning, would not bring him back.

As Linda Sue saw it, her grief was unlike the grief that Hetty and Tilya must be feeling. She didn't know for sure, but she reasoned that her sisters had seen Papa's heroic efforts to save the family in the Lodz ghetto. They were witnesses to his uncanny intelligence, his wily manoeuvres that kept them one terrifying step ahead of the Nazis. Yet the ingenious father in Lodz that Hetty and Tilya had known was not the passive, sedate Papa whom Linda Sue had known. It was as if she and her two sisters were mourning two different fathers. Nevertheless, she had honoured Papa by observing the Jewish mourning rituals. She had sat shiva for seven days with Hetty. She had not cut her hair for thirty days and refrained from listening to music in the month after Papa's death, conscious all along that what she knew of him in America was a pale reflection of his life in Poland. She lacked images of him hiding his children or stealing food for them or whatever he had done to save Hetty and Tilya. She still didn't know how they had survived.

Linda Sue could never serve as the repository of her father's memory. Impossible. But she could preserve her family's reinvented history in America. "Let's look at the family photos," she'd insist on Shabbat, often bringing the family albums to the table. "There's Terry Sue on the porch with a bobby pin in her hair," she'd say to Stacey and Josh. "Here's your bubbie," she'd remind them, pointing to a photo of their grandmother at a waterpark in the Ozarks. At every opportunity, Linda Sue shared a story, determined to carry the Berk family's recent past into the future. If her life ended tomorrow, she feared that the memory of the Berk family would be obliterated twice.

⚜

October 13, 1980

Dear me,

I can't believe that Columbus Day weekend is over. Tomorrow it's back to school with lots to get done before Thanksgiving, especially in language arts and social studies.

Heard from Peter. He sent me the most beautiful passage from a memoir by a man who survived Auschwitz. After I read it again on Sunday morning, I thought maybe I should look for a position teaching English in Poland.

I miss Papa. Losing him means that we are parentless, like orphans. I wish I knew more about what he did in the Lodz ghetto to save Mama, Hetty, and Tilya. Was he the ringleader? How did he feel about being a foreigner when he arrived here? He never really showed his emotions to us. I don't even know how he felt about losing Yeshua and Terry

Sue. But I am sure of one thing: Jews know how to mourn. The full eleven-month mourning period for a parent is genius. Still, you can't sugarcoat loss. It is what it is. More to come later in the week, once I'm happily at my teaching post with my kids again.

Toodle-oo for now,
LS.

⸭

The morning of October 14, 1980, began as most days did at Thornview Elementary. Clusters of children slowly made their way through the school's double doors, some wearing sweaters or light jackets for the first time, a sign of autumn's arrival. A few students hung back, lollygagging on the steps, reluctant to return to school after the Columbus Day break. Linda Sue had come to school early on the Tuesday after the holiday, happy to be starting a new unit in social studies, filled with a kind of shuddery relief that her lesson on the Columbus discovery story was finished, at least for now. Last week she had received a note from Jeremy Rush's mother, Diane, angry that Columbus's atrocities were never discussed in the public-school curriculum. Sitting at her desk for a few silent minutes before her students bombarded her, Linda Sue reread Diane Rush's note, which she had left in her desk drawer over the weekend to avoid dealing with it. "Our schools have a responsibility to teach the truth, and we as parents have the right to demand it," Diane Rush wrote in blue-black ink, her handwriting firm and regular. Linda Sue agreed. She vowed to stop procrastinating and make time during her lunch period to call Jeremy's mother, who was highly intelligent (a Vassar grad) and usually reasonable.

The morning progressed according to plan. Mr. Curtis, the itinerant music teacher, was scheduled to arrive in Linda Sue's Grade Five class at 10:35 a.m., just after recess, to start the far-too-long preparation for the Thanksgiving assembly.

It would include several traditional American folk songs sung in two- and three-part harmony, while, as the objectives for the fifth-grade music program stipulated, students maintained correct seated and standing postures, undoubtedly the most difficult part of the performance. Linda Sue noticed that her students were squirmy, even after they returned from the playground. She felt a momentary but intense stitch in her side, the result, she imagined, of racing up the stairs to her second-floor classroom without proper hydration. She kept the door open for a few stragglers to return to Room 210 with a minimum amount of fanfare. Linda Sue abhorred fanfare.

Just as she had achieved order in her classroom, Linda Sue heard a boom that sounded like it was coming from the first-floor lobby. Five more booms followed. They made little popping sounds, like firecrackers in the parking lot of Heman Park on the Fourth of July. When she turned her head to see what was happening, she saw a band of kids galloping down the second-floor corridor, panting and gasping for air. She wondered what the uproar was about.

Linda Sue walked over to the door where she encountered a skinny boy who seemed to have come out of nowhere. He looked vaguely familiar to her, but she had taught so many children during her years at Thornview, she wasn't sure. Sometimes when her former students dropped in to say hello, she didn't recognize them in their teenage bodies with shaved faces or pink-lipstick mouths.

"Can I help you?" she asked. "Are you here to see someone?" She expected him to say that he had come to pick up his sister for a dentist appointment or that his mother had asked him to deliver a forgotten sandwich to his younger brother. Such interruptions were typical during an ordinary school day.

The boy at the door said nothing. He seemed to have no mission. Yet, there was something in his face—the intractable stare in his eyes maybe—that made Linda Sue become rigid with fear. Sweat began to gather on the back of her neck. She extended her arm to push the door shut, but he blocked her gesture, brusquely shoving her a few steps back.

"Quick. Everyone under your desks...."

Hetty

THE NEWS OF MULTIPLE SHOOTINGS at Thornview Elementary spread through U. City by phone from relative to neighbour to friend. Rosemary Telfer, a retired school nurse, got a call from her sister, Sheila Bannerman, who lived directly across the street from the school on the corner of Dartmouth Avenue. Sheila told Rosemary that there had been some sort of shooting at Thornview. Rosemary quickly called Maureen Steiner, her neighbour on Cornell Avenue who was once the school librarian, to ask if Maureen thought they should go over to the school to help out. Their kids had graduated from Thornview years before. When they arrived, they saw children crying and visibly frightened. Teachers escorted them out of the building in a line, instructing the kids to hold onto the shoulder of the child in front of them. The principal asked Rosemary and Maureen to shepherd the children to a nearby park.

"We never thought it would happen here," said a mother of three to Rosemary and Maureen as she walked beside them. "This kind of brutal killing always seemed to happen in other places, but not in U. City." She shook her head back and forth in disbelief, her ponytail swinging. She was unaccustomed to the random horrors of the world intruding into her safe neighbourhood. None of the parents, teachers or school administrators at Thornview had any inkling that they were at the beginning of an accelerating trend in school shootings that would continue to gather force into the next century. That day Rosemary Telfer and Maureen Steiner were just helping innocent children to safety. One child stepped out of line and said, "I know some karate moves so we're okay. Follow me."

While the media rushed to Thornview and began to publicize the tragedy to a shocked nation, Marion Thomas thumbed through her study of Pruitt–Igoe, which she planned to discuss that evening in her graduate seminar on the anthropology of inner-city poverty. Several recent copies of the journal *Urban Anthropology* sat on the ottoman abutting her knees. The rock she had once picked up from the demolition of the housing project rested on top of the journals, leaving a thin coat of dust. She rose from the leather recliner to refill her coffee cup and flipped on the television to check the news and weather during her mini-break. As soon as she heard the words "multiple shootings" coupled with Thornview, her chest started to heave. She watched the television cameras panning across Thornview's Romanesque façade, listening for the names of the victims.

Weeks before, Linda Sue had invited Marion Thomas to visit her classroom. During her visit, Marion had browsed through the storybooks which Linda Sue's fifth-graders had written about themselves and proudly tacked to the bulletin board in Room 210. She had laughed at their self-portraits on the covers, particularly Karl Jackman's picture of a mad scientist with his pants falling down and Georgina Firestone's sketch of a winking wicked witch. She recalled these two students sitting next to each other in the front row. Her mind leaped to the worst case scenario. What if both of these kids were dead, their futures snuffed out?

Marion put down her cup on the stack of journals, spilling a bit of the lifeless liquid on the top one. Her clipped fingernails dug into her palms until she could see little red, half-moon indentations appear.

◈

Hetty swore up and down that she would never again host an open house for agents on the day after a long holiday weekend. Too much stress. Not enough prep time. Why was Columbus Day a state holiday anyway? Lincoln Day she understood, but Columbus Day? Ridiculous. It was just before eleven in the morning, and she already looked tired. The puffiness under her eyes and the heaviness in her gait suggested that her arthritis was acting up again. She still needed to pick up the trays of cheese and sandwiches from Dierbergs (no soup, nothing goopy), photocopy fliers at her office, tie balloons on the *For Sale* sign for her listing in Ladue Trails, do a quick check of the home (toilet seats down, dirty dishes hidden), and put on her super shiny mulberry lip gloss. Her head was spinning with details. The first agent walked through the front door at noon, just as Hetty was removing the triple sheets of cellophane from the food platters.

"Come on in," Hetty said, inspecting the agent's card. Outside, Volvos and Mercedes lined the street. A group of agents walked up the interlocking stone pathway to the front door. Carol Wilson, a high school friend entered with them. All the work was worth it, Hetty thought, anticipating an offer resulting from the increased exposure or, at the very least, the opportunity for more showings.

"Hello, Hetty," Carol Wilson said. She lifted a cube of havarti cheese to her mouth and stopped. "Can you believe what happened this morning at Thornview?"

"Excuse me," Hetty said, distracted by the flurry of agents swirling around the kitchen counter. "What did you say?"

Carol Wilson was savouring the buttery flavour of the havarti as she strolled through the home's combined living/ dining room. Hetty followed her. "What happened at Thornview?" she asked.

"There's been some kind of mass shooting," Carol Wilson said. She eyed the rustic hutch against the wall, filled with country French dinnerware.

Hetty returned to the kitchen to phone Thornview, although she was positive that Linda Sue was unharmed. American schools, in her experience, were hardly fertile ground for catastrophes, at least not compared to what she and Tilya had witnessed in Lodz. Besides, it seemed unlikely that the Berks would be hit with another tragedy in their lifetimes. They had endured more than their share, she assured herself as she waited for someone to answer at Thornview.

"I'd better drive down there to make sure Linda Sue is okay," she said to Carol Wilson. "Would you mind locking up and returning the key to my office? And take the leftovers home," she said over her shoulder.

By the time Hetty arrived at the school, the building was taped off as a crime scene. Hetty knew some of the younger teachers who were not only colleagues of Linda Sue's but also her workout buddies, travel companions, and confidants. One of them spotted Hetty immediately and took her inside the school. Hetty felt herself becoming irritable. All she needed to know was that her sister was safe. Then she planned to drive her home, make her a cup of tea, and return to her office in time to meet her three o'clock client. She walked into Room 210 with arms extended, ready to hug Linda Sue and say I love you. When she saw her lying on the floor in a pool of blood, she gasped and fell to the ground next to her.

❖

Overnight Thornview Elementary became a public shrine. Visitors from all over St. Louis County came to pay their respects and to leave an avalanche of candles, bouquets, wreaths, and poems. The following week a memorial service was organized by the governor of Missouri in the U. City High football stadium across the street from Thornview. The governor released rainbow-coloured balloons into the air, one for each of the deceased, bearing his or her name. In the months to come, students were not allowed to return to the school. The building remained mired in disrepair from the shootings, and the students were too troubled to re-enter their terrorized school, not to mention trying to resume learning there. They were sent to Flynn Park or Pershing Elementary for the rest of the school term. Some parents, sensing a pervasive danger, insisted on home schooling their children. They suspected that tragedy could indeed strike twice, even in an idyllic community like U. City where people trusted each other, often didn't lock their front doors, and regularly watched out for each other's children.

⬧

October 14, 1980

Dear Diary,

Here's the coverage of the school shooting from the *Post Dispatch*.

October 15, 1980—University City, Mo. A shooting rampage in this quiet suburb of St. Louis on Tuesday morning left fourteen people dead, including ten children killed inside Thornview Elementary School, authorities said.

The dead included the suspected gunman, whom law enforcement officers identified as Ryan Metcalf, 18. Police found three guns: a .223 caliber "Bushmaster" rifle and two pistols, a Sig Sauer and a Glock in his car.

At the school, authorities confirmed that Ryan Metcalf shot and killed three adults—including the school's principal, Alison Rogers—and ten children. They were shot in two different classrooms in the school.

Police were called to the school shortly after 10:30 a.m., and officers searched the classrooms for a shooter. When they found the shooter, he was dead by his own hand. He was wearing a green vest over a polo shirt, black fingerless gloves, and orange earplugs. No officer fired a shot.

Among the dead were two teachers, Mr. G. Curtis, an itinerant music teacher, and Miss Linda Sue Berk, a fifth-grade teacher, according to law enforcement sources. Press reports stated that Berk had been at Thornview Elementary for six years. "She was always enthusiastic, always smiling, always ready to do anything for her students," said Janice Dodds, a former secretary of the school's Parent Teacher Association. In a phone interview, she recalled Miss Berk hugging the children at the start of the school year. "She wanted them to do well, but she also wanted them to have fun."

Children who were evacuated from the school were told to keep their eyes closed until they were outside the building. Over the course of the day, police accounted for every child who attended the school, tracking down even those who were absent because of illness. One child was taken to St. Louis Children's Hospital, where she died later that night of gunshot wounds.

I told Josh today. He's inconsolable.

He'll be the one to say kaddish for her because he's the only male Berk left. Thank G-d that Mama and Papa are not alive. This would have killed them. They lived only for their children. How many can you lose before you decide to depart yourself? One is enough. No, one is too many. And the loss of Yeshua, Terry Sue, and now Linda Sue is beyond imaginable. I feel so alone, so lifeless that I'd like to follow my sisters to the grave.

Always,
Hetty

Toni

IN THE WAKE OF THE MISSOURI school shooting, a group of U. City parents founded a grassroots organization called Rise Again. It encouraged the community to develop a sense of resilience and hope, rather than becoming trapped in feelings of helplessness and fear. They set up their meeting space in a donated storefront located in the Delmar Loop, not far from the Berks' first apartment in St. Louis. Artwork sent by children from across America adorned the walls. Framed, poster-size photos of the victims, including a picture of an exuberant Linda Sue, hung over the desks in the office. She was reclining in a chaise lounge by a swimming pool, wearing a hot pink tank top and white shorts. Her toenails were painted a bold, fun fuchsia.

Scattered on the tables at Rise Again were pamphlets describing foundations established by grieving families. Printed on the front of every pamphlet was a rifle inside a circle with a thick black line diagonally across it. The prohibitory message below the graphic read *Ban Assault Weapons Now*. Rise Again bumper stickers rested on a nearby shelf with the motto: *Imagine a future free of gun violence*. In the far corner of the office, an aging, local musician who once played in Gaslight Square strummed a plaintive classical guitar solo.

Toni sat on the edge of her seat at another table. She had taken a mid-semester leave from her teaching position in New

York to deal with her sister's death and to advocate for an end to gun violence. She had travelled often to Washington to lobby lawmakers on the passage of a gun control law. ("Good luck with that," Hetty had said when she heard of Toni's latest campaign.) Toni stared at the enlarged image of Linda Sue. So much goodness wiped out by the bullet of a gun.

She put her head down on the table top but only rested for a few seconds. She lifted her eyes, swimming in tears, and squinted at Linda Sue again, overcome by memories of her as a young kid with a million questions. What was Lodz like? Did you and Hetty sleep in the same bed? Did Mama make kasha varnishkes for you in Lodz, like she does for us in St. Louis? Tell me, Linda Sue would say to her. What's the big secret? Despite her grief, Toni was filled with a roar of energy. She felt enormous, the size of the whole storefront, exploding with purpose in her pregnant body.

"We can stop gun violence. We must," she said aloud to the empty chair next to her just before she rose to address the audience of supporters.

"Friends, neighbors and residents from across St. Louis, tonight I stand before you in the office of Rise Again to ask for your help. A number of us gathered here are in mourning for the losses we suffered at Thornview Elementary School about a month ago. Grief, it turns out, is a space that you don't really recognize until you inhabit it yourself."

Toni nodded at Diane Rush, mother of Jeremy, and the parents of Georgina Firestone, who were sitting close to the podium set up in the storefront.

"I am one of those people who lost a family member on October 14. My youngest sister, Linda Sue Berk was killed in her classroom, protecting the children she loved. She was just thirty-two years old. Who on earth would believe that I, born in Poland, a child survivor of the Holocaust, would outlive my youngest sister, who was born here? I was supposed to die of typhus in the Lodz ghetto, where we were incarcerated, or be gassed to death in Auschwitz. Instead my oldest sister Hetty and I have ended up lowering Linda Sue into a grave on Hanley Road in the middle of what our parents called nowhere.

"Like my sister, Linda Sue, I am a teacher. A shooting in a school, a sanctuary of learning, a safe haven, appalls me. A school rampage evokes in me the most profound outrage, as I am sure it does in you. Unnecessary cruelty and brutality are horrible enough, but when innocent children are the victims, their young lives cut short, we cannot remain silent. And what's worse, I'm beginning to think that if such violence can happen in a school, it can happen in movie theatres, restaurants, shopping malls. Because violence is ubiquitous. It's always brewing, like arsenic steeping in a pot of bitter tea." She paused and leaned into the crowd.

"But friends, that's not how I remember U. City. The truth is I can recall only one violent incident growing up here. Linda Sue would have been able to describe the incident better than I can because it involved some of her high school buddies who were attacked by a gang of knife-wielding, gun-toting boys on a summer night in Heman Park. One of her friends nearly lost his eye when a bullet grazed his temple. Others were slashed and hospitalized."

For a moment, Toni returned to that incident in Heman Park, which hadn't crossed her mind in years. The terror that Mama and Papa had felt that night still reverberated. Mama had said, "It shouldn't happen here to such nice Jewish boys." One of them became a rabbi. After that, Linda Sue had been forbidden to go to the park after five in the afternoon, and Terry Sue had never been allowed go with her.

"I feel obligated to repeat the obvious: there are too many guns in America. We can't delude ourselves into thinking that school shootings and gun violence will ever end without taking action to stop them. Gun laws, or anything that thwarts shooters from getting their hands on guns, will make it harder to perpetrate a massacre like the one that happened at Thornview Elementary. But let's be honest: a determined person will find a way. That's why gun control laws, though necessary, are not sufficient. Implementing these laws is certainly not the only step we must take. We need a theory and a comprehensive plan."

"We need action." The crowd shouted back.

"We need action—yes—but we also need a theory if we want to make real change."

Toni stepped away from the podium. She tugged on her shirt, which was stretched tightly across her protruding belly, and scanned the faces in the audience. Hetty wasn't among them. Hands were flying in the air. Speaker after speaker urged immediate action. Someone started a petition that read *We demand gun control now!* and circulated the sheet of paper up and down the rows for signatures. Toni rubbed the temple at the side of her head. She could be forgiven if her speech at Rise Again failed in its plea for a multi-pronged approach to rampage school shootings. She seemed to be the outlier in the room, possibly the only person there that needed a theory—concepts, definitions, propositions, research questions, evidence—to grasp what appeared utterly random and inexplicable.

⸭

November 12, 1980

So here's the beginning of my grant application on school shootings. It's just about the only thing I'm thinking about these days.

Areas for investigation:
- *Psychological profile of shooter: loner, socially awkward, previous criminal involvement, mental illness?*

- *Family background: class, race, single-parent or two-parent family?*
- *Setting: rural vs. urban, community with low crime rate vs. high crime rate?*
- *Gender: why male? Images of masculinity in media*
- *Contributing factors: bullying, violence in media, access to guns, other?*
- *Why schools?*
- *Why my sister? Why did Linda Sue have to die? Why did any of those kids have to die?*

Sisterhood forever,
Toni

Hetty

HETTY TRIED EVERYTHING she could imagine to halt her depression, briefly taking up yoga and swallowing increased amounts of vitamin D as well as saffron supplements. On Tilya's recommendation, she made an appointment to see George Rosen, a psychotherapist whose office was located in the medical building on Delmar. She climbed the stairs to his third-floor office dreading their meeting, but hopeful that her grief would dissipate as a result of their sessions. The notion of exposing herself and revealing family secrets terrified her. Berks didn't divulge what was locked up. In the weeks ahead, however, she was able to loosen the grip of those ironclad handcuffs she normally wore.

"How are you feeling today," George asked at the beginning of each session. She liked the earnest way he focused on her. She didn't need to compete with anyone or anything for his attention.

"I'm still sleeping way too much," she said.

"Maybe your dreams are helping you deal with the death of Linda Sue and Terry Sue, and reaching further back, the disappearance of your brother Yeshua. Those losses may be too painful to hold in your conscious mind."

She stared blankly at him. "Am I ever going to feel better?"

George beamed at her. "It takes time."

❖

Hetty gradually regained momentum, though she procrastinated over the sale of Papa's house, waiting for real estate values to increase in local strength after a long run of slumping prices. She upgraded the counters and installed glossy hardwood flooring in the kitchen, then priced the house high without consulting Tilya. Reversing her previous inclination, she was in no hurry to sell now that her father was dead. Although she had never been the type of agent that did real estate between tennis games, she wasn't an aggressive agent topping a million bucks a year in sales either. Far from it. Factoring in the impact of the shooting spree at Thornview, a mere two blocks away from the Papa's house on Tulane, she reckoned that timing was not in her favour.

Yet it was undeniable that residents of U. City, an increasingly mixed community, demonstrated a remarkable ability to rally together and restore a sense of safety to the neighbourhood. Some armed themselves with .45 calibre hand guns, which they concealed under handkerchiefs in their top dresser drawers. Others bought assault rifles, which they stored in their garages next to their lawnmowers. The good news was that Thornview Elementary was slated to reopen after the March break. Soon children would be walking to school again, more closely chaperoned by parents than in the carefree past.

One morning, in the week before Thanksgiving, when Hetty was still euphoric that Reagan had been elected president, she walked to the mailbox at the end of her driveway with a particular spring in her step. No other Berk had ever voted Republican. (Mama didn't count because she never voted, regardless of who was running or what they were running for.) Nevertheless, Hetty cast her ballot for the GOP anticipating economic recovery. She was daydreaming about an April sale of Papa's house as she opened the mailbox and pulled out a large envelope with Josh's return address on it.

Up the curved walkway she scurried, noticing a broken brick at the edge of the path close to the house. She was running late for her first client. Inside, she ripped open the envelope and put the catalogue of Josh's photography exhibit on the kitchen counter. She read the title, then shuddered: *As I Remember Him.*

Later that night, it took Hetty less than a minute to recognize Josh in each photographic portrait in the catalogue. All of the portraits featured him in costumes, makeup, and hair styles depicting him as Yeshua Berkowicz. He used various props to re-enact the imagined life of his namesake: baby Yeshua wearing a bib, sitting with one tubby leg tucked under the other and a rattle in his hand; three-year-old Yeshua, a soft curl falling on his forehead, wearing shorts, with a sail boat on his lap; seven-year-old Yeshua in a mask for Purim; ten-year-old Yeshua at a school desk holding a thick book; thirteen-year-old Yeshua wearing a suit, bowtie and *tallit* at his Bar Mitzvah; nineteen-year-old Yeshua with short hair in a soldier's uniform; twenty-two-year-old Yeshua under the *chuppah* at his wedding; twenty-four-year-old Yeshua cradling his son at the ritual circumcision.

Hetty turned the pages of the softcover catalogue until she nodded off, and it dropped onto her chest. She'd call Josh to congratulate him in the morning.

❖

November 21, 1980

Dear Diary,

Who is this lost boy who grows into manhood in Josh's catalogue? He's not my real brother Yeshua. He never had a Bar Mitzvah or a wedding. The Nazis made sure of that. Mama and Papa would have cried a river if they had seen Josh's catalogue. I can barely look at it myself. If I've learned one thing in therapy, it's this. There's no cure for the Holocaust.

Josh can't save my murdered brother no matter how creatively he keeps his memory alive. Yeshua is not coming back. Okay, maybe I'm being too hard on Josh. There might very well be a human urge to give shape to what is gone. I need to ask George about that. Therapists know these kinds of things.

Always,
Hetty

Toni

GALAXY PUT HIS HEAD on Toni's pillow, so close to her face that she felt his cold nose touching her nostrils. Her cat and a small carry-on bag were the only possessions that Toni had taken from her tenement on East 27th Street when she left for Linda Sue's funeral. More than a month later, she suspected that she would never go back to her old walk-up with the quaint bathtub and the smell of fried liver and onions in the stairwell. How was she going to schlep a baby carriage up and down five flights of stairs? Where was the baby going to sleep in an apartment the size of a shoebox? How was she going to do tons of the baby's laundry without a washer and dryer? Maybe in the sink. The longer she stayed in U. City—living in Linda Sue's house and eating the food that had been left in her fridge, discarding wilting lettuce and squishy cucumbers one day at a time—the more Toni realized that her youngest sister's death was a watershed moment for her. She stroked Galaxy, who refused to cease his meowing. "But even Linda Sue's death can't just be a personal thing," she said to Galaxy as he pawed her arm for breakfast. "That's not how change happens, Mr. Hungry Kid Cat."

Before replenishing the cat's bowl of food, before brushing her teeth or peeing, she phoned her friend Cameron in New York to ask him to pack up her apartment and ship her few belongings to St. Louis. "You can keep the spider plant," she said. "Or you can bring it when you come to see the baby." On the same morning, she applied for an extension of her emergency leave from the university and disconnected her Manhattan phone line.

"I'm not going back," Toni said when Marion arrived about an hour later with the final draft of their grant proposal titled "The Root Causes and Consequences of School Shootings." "I've decided to take a maternity leave. It's unlikely that I'll ever return to New York. "

"Are you sure?" asked Marion, placing the proposal on Linda Sue's kitchen table. "It takes me longer to buy a pair of socks at the mall than for you to upend your entire life."

"Well, that's grief for you. It's like a fog so dense that you can't see your way out of it anymore." She thumbed through the proposal to find the literature review that Marion had prepared, noting that the field was ripe for a major theoretical breakthrough. Theirs. She furrowed her brows. "Sometimes the only way through grief is to act. I should know."

Marion closed her eyes and sighed while Toni sliced bagels and toasted them for their breakfast. For as long as she had known Toni, she had been struck by her feisty confidence. This was a woman whose sense of mission superseded everything else. That uncompromising resolve bound them together.

"Okay," Marion said. A note of warning crept into her voice. "Taking action is one response, but don't think for one minute that it replaces grieving for Linda Sue." Marion swept crumbs off the proposal and buttered her bagel. She had begun to feel at home in this kitchen so redolent with the smell of Linda Sue's spices and dish soap. Marion got up to make herself a cup of tea instead of waiting to be served. She shifted items around in the fridge until she found the raspberry jam, then examined the expiry date on the carton of milk. On the counter, she noticed a pair of kitchen scissors with handles that looked like an animal's small ears. A cute pink case in the shape of a giraffe with big brown spots protected the blades.

"Where did your sister get these funny scissors?" Marion said.

"I sent them to her from Japan. They were a gift from Kazuo," Toni said. "I thought Linda Sue would get a kick out of them."

"What kind of gift is a pair of giraffe scissors?" Marion asked. "If you don't mind my curiosity, was this guy trying to tell you something or what?"

Toni looked down and patted her ballooning stomach. She could no longer see her toes. "It was his way of being intimate," she said, taking a short breath. "You know, one of those whimsical kind of things guys do."

"Does this whimsical guy of yours know you're pregnant? Does anyone over there know?"

"Doubtful."

"Doubtful?"

"I'm not telling them."

"I'm not either." Marion picked up the giraffe scissors and pretended to snip something. "You'll have to come up with a damn good explanation for these crazy scissors because one day, when you are least expecting it, the kid will ask you about them."

When Lynn K. Berk—K for short—was born at the St. Louis Jewish Hospital, the same hospital where Terry Sue and Linda Sue had been born decades before, Toni announced proudly that her pudgy baby with inquisitive brown eyes, a shock of straight black hair, and a large, swollen penis, was a fatherless child whose paternity would forever be ambiguous, as would his/her gender, religion, race, and ethnicity. She prevailed upon her niece Stacey to remove her cherry dress from its frame, still hanging on the wall in Frontenac, and bequeath her most cherished piece of clothing to cousin K to wear on special occasions, namely Passover Seders and Buddha's birthday. (Toni would eventually celebrate Mother's Day, having adjusted her thinking while spending her nights pacing the hallowed halls of motherhood with a sleep-averse baby.)

One mild winter afternoon, when K slept soundly in Linda Sue's former study, Toni seized the moment to dash off a Letter to the Editor of the *St. Louis Post Dispatch* on the dire need for gun control. Her typewriter, surrounded by diapers and baby wipes on top of Linda Sue's old desk, hummed with urgency. She glanced at the crib hugging the outside wall of the study and eyed Linda Sue's books, which had been left untouched since her death. Wrap up this letter fast, she admonished herself, before K begins to shriek. She smelled the baby's dirty diaper across the room. His chubby legs moved restlessly in his snug yellow cotton sleeper. Without thinking, she signed the letter *Zysla Berkowicz.*

⚜

As the months passed, Tilya settled into Linda Sue's house which was not far from her parents' home on Tulane. She strolled past the old place daily with K on their morning walks. Each time they reached it, she made a full stop. She squatted beside the baby and looked directly into his luminous eyes, their foreheads nearly touching. In a small voice, she told the burbling infant that his grandparents once lived here, regretful that he would never know them.

Since K's birth, Toni felt closer to her parents than at any previous time she could recall. She often surprised herself by singing a Yiddish song as she clapped K's plump hands together. *Patshe, patshe kikhelekh*, she crooned to him in front of Mama and Papa's house. And when she pinched the baby's rosy cheek on the last word of the lullaby—it took her a moment to remember that *bekelekh* meant cheeks in Yiddish—she imagined the touch of Mama's skeletal fingers on her skin in the ghetto. Rocking K to sleep at night, she recounted stories that her parents had told her about aunts and uncles living in Lodz and Warsaw before the Nazis had occupied Poland. Fearing that her Polish past was slipping away, Toni tried to tether her son to what she had lost, the tales told in unfinished sentences and the stories never written down. Oddly, she understood their trauma more now than she had when they were alive. Something had shifted in her, impelling her to move forward, like any activist worth her salt would.

When an opportunity arose, Toni jumped at the chance to investigate a tip from her friend Cameron, whose colleague at Yale was also a child of Holocaust survivors. Over dinner together in New York, the colleague had alluded to the Holocaust Survivors' Video Archive, which was under development in New Haven. By the next day, Cam had relayed the information to Toni, who phoned Hetty.

"We must become involved in this project," Toni said. "They are collecting and recording Holocaust witness testimonies from individuals with first-hand experience. That's us." She could barely contain her excitement, ready, as never before, to become the voice of Mama and Papa's memories.

"Do we have to talk about this now?" Hetty was engrossed in an offer of purchase, obsessing at the moment over the legalese in the contract. "Can't it wait a couple of hours? Or centuries?"

"Not really. They're looking for survivors, bystanders, resisters, liberators, and anyone who was in hiding." Toni rolled a ball toward K with her foot and puckered her lips, as if to throw a kiss to the baby, who was playing with a squeaky rubber doll on the floor. "Don't you want to keep their memory alive? You were older and remember more of what happened than I do."

"You and this memory business," Hetty said, reluctant to embrace her sister's latest cause. Despite Toni's passionate pleas, Hetty felt a niggling doubt, a distrust of going public about their past in Poland. She had forced herself to confide in her therapist George, but giving testimony to strangers took trust to a new level. She could hear Mama warning her to be silent because evil always lurked around the corner. Trying to squelch Toni's enthusiasm, she said, "What difference do any of our memories make anyway?"

"Don't you see that fewer and fewer people who survived the war are left? If we don't come forward to talk about the Holocaust, the deniers will. Don't you care?"

"I care. I care," Hetty said. "Call me later."

True to form, Toni persisted and prevailed. In a matter of months, Hetty and Toni, with baby K in tow, were on their way to New Haven. Josh and Stacey had agreed to join them to hear the recording of their mother's testimony. They realized it was impossible for her to talk directly to them about what had happened. It was somehow easier for Hetty to add her account to the testimonies generated in thirty-seven affiliated projects across North America, South America, Europe, and Israel than to sit down in their spacious Frontenac family room and tell her children what happened. Rightly or wrongly, she had always tried to prevent the Holocaust from rippling through their lives, but she had failed.

Once the recording of her testimony began, Hetty needed little prodding. Fragmentary bits of her childhood spilled out, as if she had suddenly found the lost key to her safety deposit box at the bank.

She testified: "Even young children were dispatched to procure food. Once I was sent to the black market for some potatoes. I took the Star of David from my coat and wandered around saying, 'Heil Hitler!' as loudly as I could. After I bought the potatoes, I got on the tram to go back to our apartment. When the conductor came around, I reached into my pocket to get some coins. And as I took out my money, the Star of David fell out. A young man was nearby. He put his boot down so that conductor couldn't see that I was Jewish. He saved my life."

"You were great," Stacey said, smiling at Hetty at the conclusion of the first recording session. She'd never seen her mother's face so lit up and vibrant.

"I wish Aunt Linda had been here," Josh said. "She would have been very proud of you."

Toni put her arm around Hetty's shoulder and kissed the side of her head. She started to tell her they would always be inseparable sisters, but the words became impossible to say. They breathed together for a minute before K started to wiggle in his baby carrier and open his mouth, demanding to eat.

⬥

A severe weather warning was in effect when the Berks returned to St. Louis. Toni remembered Mama's fear of tornadoes, which perhaps wasn't as irrational as she had once supposed. Hetty called to remind her that more tornado fatalities occurred in the St. Louis area than in any other city in the United States. "Go to the basement," Hetty told her. "The interior part." Toni put down the receiver, discounting every word Hetty said. After a few minutes she phoned Marion.

"Any news on the funding of our project on gun violence and shootings in schools?" Toni asked. It's been quite a while since we applied."

"Not yet." Marion said, aware of the impatience in Toni's voice. "Hang up," Marion advised her. "And go to the basement. Girl, don't you know a tornado is coming?"

A couple of days later, while changing K on Linda Sue's desk, Toni opened the top drawer in search of the Penaten she used to protect K's bum from diaper rash. She fumbled around in the shallow drawer with one hand, holding the baby in place with the other. She couldn't find the tin. *What decent mother wanted to be caught without the thick white cream when irritation inflamed her baby's tuchas?* Toni felt a pang of guilt. That would be tantamount to child abuse. She reached to the very back of the drawer, trying to recall the last time she had used the cream, but the Penaten tin was definitely gone. Toni ran her hand methodically across the entire back of the drawer again. In the corner, she touched something smooth and cool. She pulled it out and saw that it was a blue notebook with a plastic Cerlox binding. *All About Me* was the title scrawled across the cover. *Linda Sue Berk* was written underneath it. When K started to squirm, Toni dropped Linda Sue's diary on the floor, where it remained until K settled into sleep later in the evening.

With her lower back aching from exhaustion and her brain feeling like a bowl of mush, Toni strained to pick up Linda Sue's diary. Turning the notebook over in her hands, she remembered the day she had offered the diaries to her sisters. She thumbed through it, skimming a few passages. These were the only written words her baby sister had left behind—all that remained of her innermost thoughts and musings. Toni smoothed her hand over the notebook as if it were a precious object that held a deep family secret. From the beginning, Toni had intended to deposit all three of their diaries into a Holocaust archive somewhere. That's why she had given her sisters the notebooks in the first place. She thought a researcher might someday find their experiences of growing up in a family of Holocaust survivors informative, even publishable. The diaries, Toni had thought, would add to an understanding of how traumas, such as the Holocaust, are passed down from parents to children. Toni could see at least one doctoral thesis emerging on that topic from the blue, red, and avocado green diaries of the Berk sisters, if not a whole field of study. She brought Linda Sue's blue diary to her cheek. Nope. She loved her sister too much to violate her privacy like that without permission.

Besides, Toni no longer had the urge to contribute to scholarly research in the same way that she once did. The emerging academic study of the "intergenerational transmission of trauma in second- and third-generation Holocaust survivors" appealed to her less and less. Toni was ready to accept her family's history without having it turned into a scholarly book on inherited trauma or a journal article or an area for further investigation. She didn't need the diaries as evidence of her family's Holocaust legacy or anything else. *We are who we are*, she assured herself. If their story evaded completion and the full details of their survival remained a mystery, so be it.

Toni returned Linda Sue's diary to the desk drawer where her sister had left it. The next day, she and K walked up to the drugstore on North and South Road at Delmar to buy a new tin of soothing cream for K's dimpled, chapped bum.

On a summer day, long after Papa's house had sold and Josh's photographs of the Lodz ghetto had been exhibited all over the world, Toni held a poem slip that she had created in one hand and opened the back door for barefooted K with the other hand. The noonday sun peeked through the clouds, making the summer heat in U. City feel unbearably humid. A breeze picked up. Toni smelled something earthy, like a sweet, pungent zing to her nostrils. Before attaching the slip of paper to the closest sycamore tree, she told K that the words were written by a great man named Elie Wiesel. who had seen many bad things and had the courage to write about what he saw.

"Someone named Piotr sent these words to your Aunt Linda Sue," she said. "I read them in a letter that slipped out of her diary.

Never shall I forget that smoke.
Never shall I forget the small faces of the children
whose bodies I saw
transformed into smoke under a silent sky.

She brushed her lips against the words and kissed her child's forehead. The first drops of rain smeared the ink on the poem slip. Soon Toni and K were drenched in the gentle rainfall, in its promise of hope, beyond all shadows.

Acknowledgements

Memory's Shadow is a novella about sisters and sisterhood. The book could have no better home than at Inanna Publications, a pioneering Canadian feminist press. In the forty-plus years since its founding, Inanna has nurtured so many women writers and given voice to disenfranchised and marginalized women, as well as emerging writers and established authors. I am proud to be one of them. I am indebted to Luciana Ricciutelli, the late editor-in-chief of Inanna Publications for her steadfast commitment to my work and the warmth of her embrace. I also want to thank Renée Knapp at Inanna for her enthusiastic and gracious support throughout the publishing process.

I am grateful to my St. Louis family who keep me tethered to the past and grounded in the present, particularly my brother Les Benick and his wife Judie. My beloved cousins Sondra Baron and Sally Zimmerman mean the world to me. I will never forget Marci Zimmerman whose heroic courage and determination are a constant reminder of how to break barriers.

In Toronto, I am fortunate to have a network of women writers who generously share resources and offer guidance. Thank you Maria Meindl for your mentoring over the years and Marianne Apostolides who first believed in this project. My dear friend Susan Charney is a wellspring of encouragement. Phyllis Greenberg and Naomi Alboim lift my spirits. I am blessed to have a family that expands my understanding of the world, particularly my daughters-in-law, Kristin Olson and Asha Forrester and the Siemiatycki clan. I have benefitted from conversations with Keiko Burke about the ripple of history through our lives and the terrain of memory. Above all, I thank my wonderful husband Myer and our sons Matti and Elliot for their abiding love and goodness. Naiya, Olly, Jacob, Isobel, and Tristan David—our next generation—give me a reason to get up in the morning and write.

Photo: Melanie Gordon Photography

Gail Benick is a Toronto author and educator. Her career as a professor in the Faculty of Humanities and Social Sciences at Sheridan College in Oakville, Ontario, spanned more than three decades. Her debut novella, *The Girl Who Was Born That Way*, was published in 2015. http://www.gailbenick.com/